Multicultural

D1483570

Light
Chaser

Zahra Omar Shansab

Publisher Page
an imprint of Headline Books, Inc.
Terra Alta, WV

Light Chaser

by Zahra Omar Shansab

To order additional copies of this book or for book publishing information, or to contact the author:

Headline Books, Inc.
P.O. Box 52
Terra Alta, WV 26764
www.HeadlineBooks.com

Tel: 304-789-3001
Email: mybook@headlinebooks.com

Publisher Page is an imprint of Headline Books

ISBN: 9781951556358

Library of Congress Control Number: 2021940136

PRINTED IN THE UNITED STATES OF AMERICA

For my beloved father,
You will always be my guiding light.

1

Pari sat patiently on the ledge of the doorway facing the courtyard. She was waiting for the distant sounds of the explosions to subside. "I wonder whose village is getting bombed today," she said out loud. "Afghanistan is a cursed land. Only God can break this curse." Her father's words echoed in her ears. "Does God even care anymore?" Pari mumbled while she traced an ambiguous shape on the dusty ground with the tip of her finger.

Pari remembered a day in her second-grade class when the girls were asked to draw and color the map of the country. Pari had colored her map all in red. Her grandfather had often said he wouldn't be surprised if the color of the soil would also turn red after so many years of war and bloodshed. The teacher was not amused by Pari's explanation. She pulled Pari by the ear and made her stand in the corner of the classroom for the rest of the day. Then she took away Pari's red pencil, never returning it. Second grade was so long ago, thought Pari. Even though her mischievous acts got her in trouble many times, she still missed her school and her friends terribly. But the thought of school and learning was no longer a possibility for girls like her.

As soon as the thunderous booms of the explosions gave way to silence, a melodious chirping of the birds filled the crisp fall air. Pari listened intently. She held her breath, trying not to miss any whistles or chirps. She looked at the leaves swaying gently. The branches danced in perfect synch with the singing of the birds. She loved how the warmth of the sun stroked her face. It felt like the wings of an angel, she thought, touching her face.

Closing her eyes, she turned her face to the sun, and taking a deep breath, she opened them. The brightness blinded her. She raised her hand, trying to shield her face from the vibrant rays. "I see blood flowing through my veins," Pari whispered softly. It's as red as the tulips. Red as my mother's favorite *chador* (headscarf) she wore on special occasions." Her fingers danced around in the air, trying to catch the sun rays.

"What are you doing, Pari?" her mother's voice pierced through her thoughts. "Why are you just sitting there and wiggling your fingers? Get up and help me sweep the room."

Pari continued to drift away with her thoughts as she gazed at the clouds and ignored her mother's scolding. At that point, she had already tuned her mother completely out.

She loved how the clouds changed into different shapes. Sometimes they looked like herds of white, fluffy sheep ushered around by the wind; sometimes, they looked like round cotton balls dancing around; and sometimes they just looked like her grandfather's long unruly beard.

The thought of her grandfather made her spring up to her feet. She took off, running across the deep burgundy carpet with intricate designs framed into several squares. As she was running across the small living room, she jumped and hopped over those squares. When she was much younger, she hopscotched on the carpet, jumping from one square to another and skipping the other. Sometimes she didn't have any reasons or rules for all that jumping, but it sure felt good every time. As she jumped over the last square on her way out of the living room, her mother's loud scream stopped her in her tracks.

"What is wrong with you? When will you ever grow up? You are no longer a little girl, Pari. For God's sake! You are almost thirteen. I was not much older when I was married off and had to assume household responsibilities."

"I would rather get hit by a stray bullet. There is definitely no shortage of those around here," Pari said, chuckling at her mother.

Pari's mother slapped her forehead in despair as she slumped down on the floor. Pari giggled out loud and hurried along the dark and narrow hallway that led to her grandfather's little room.

"I am so sorry, Grandfather. I lost track of time." She yelled as she pushed the door open.

Her grandfather lay on a thin mattress stretched along the mud wall of the room. He flashed her a toothless smile. Sunshine sneaked through a small window, illuminating her grandfather's long, white beard. *It almost looked silvery,* Pari thought. She held her grandfather's hand between hers and knelt down by his side.

"Grandfather, do you know how beautiful it is outside?" Pari planted a kiss on the back of his rough and wrinkled hand and before he could respond, she continued, "I am going to take you out to the yard. You will love the fresh air!"

Her grandfather groaned and coughed as he lifted his fragile body up on his elbows. Pari put her hand underneath his skinny back and gave him a push helping him to sit up. As soon as he sat up and got a break from coughing, he looked at Pari and patted her head with affection.

"I have always known that you would be my little angel who would watch over me," he said, "You are my little fairy. Just like your name." He sighed in pain as he continued. "The night that you were born, the sky was so clear and dotted with thousands of glittering stars. Your father and I were waiting outside and praying for a safe delivery. I looked up at the sky and asked your father if I could choose a name if it was going to be a girl."

Pari smiled at her grandfather and squeezed his hands softly between hers. She had heard this story a hundred times before. But each time she listened with eagerness, knowing it made her grandfather happy.

Her grandfather smiled as he proudly continued, "And when you were born, I named you my little Pari (fairy). That night, among the bright stars, I imagined you flying around with glowing wings as bright as the moon."

"Or as bright as the wings of the firefly?" Pari asked.

"No, brighter! It felt like the dark sky had plucked the moon and placed it in our arms. We could not stop staring at you. Your father loved you so much."

As he spoke, a dark cloud of sadness and pain slowly covered his face. He shielded his face with both hands as if to hide from the ghost of the past.

"I wish I could have saved your father that unfortunate day," he said, "I don't know why God chose to save me and took my son."

Pari's grandfather rested his head against the mud wall and began to sob softly. By now, Pari was used to this bitter routine as her grandfather often cried with remorse. She hugged him as cautiously as she could. Lately, her grandfather's frail body had begun to worry her. Hugging him felt like embracing a bag of bones. She looked at his weak and fragile body and tried not to look at his leg, the leg that was missing from the knee down.

2

Pari sat next to her mother by the warm stove, thinking about that day two years ago, a day that had started just like any other day. She remembered how eagerly she watched as her mother cooked the potato soup. She loved how her mother's green eyes sparkled as the stove's heat caressed her chapped, dry skin. Her mother was so beautiful, she thought. All the women in the village were envious of her milky -white skin and emerald green eyes. Pari always wished that she had inherited her mother's pretty eyes. When Pari was younger, she sometimes would stand on a wobbly wooden stool to reach the mirror, which hung on the mud wall of her parent's room. She always struggled to balance herself on the rickety stool as she examined her features. She spent a lot of time looking at her almond-shaped brown eyes, thin nose, oval face, and black curly hair. And she always concluded that she would never be as beautiful as her mother.

Her mother often scolded her about her unkempt appearance and wild hair covering her face. Every morning, her mother made her sit on the floor and combed the knots out of her hair. Her mother made sure that the process was not a pleasant one. Pari cried and complained as her mother's scolding bombarded her ears. She admonished her that the braids better be intact by the end of the day. But as soon as Pari was freed from the claws of her mother, she would take off shaking her head violently from side to side. "Why do I have to look neat?" she would say in desperation to herself. "I can no longer go to school anyway! I don't care if I look like a wild animal. Neither do I care if my hair looks like a broom." Pari started to choke up but fought the tears back as she continued her outburst. "I want to go to school. I want to have books to read and do homework just like I used to. I hate this!"

Pari ran towards the barberry bush. As soon as she crawled underneath it, she burst out in tears. She was very angry and she did not even care if the barberry bush's long thorns scratched her head and face. She tagged angrily at her hair in an effort to set them free from the thorns and little oval leaves.

As soon as she had crawled deep inside the bush and was concealed from her mother's view, Pari rested her head between her knees and continued to cry. She watched her tears drop on the dusty ground dissolving quickly. "Thirsty monster you are," she said out loud,

pointing to the ground. "Look at how quickly you soak up my tears."

She wiped her nose on the hem of her dress and went on crying, but now she did so softly. She felt worn out and her throat was irritated. She rested her chin on her knee and watched an ant climb up her toe. "What do you want?" she mumbled. "I can squash you in a second." She remembered how her teacher would compare humans to ants, trying to teach them about the vastness of the universe. She would explain how small human beings were compared to its size. And she added God had created everything.

Pari looked closer at the ant as it slowly made its way to the back of her bare foot. She watched its antenna wiggle back and forth as two more ants marched behind it. As she reached out to swat at them, she imagined them having human faces attached to their little bodies, looking up at her and begging her not to be harmed. She hesitated, pondered, and then very gingerly picked them up and set them on the ground. "Go on home now," Pari whispered. "I would not want a giant to trample on me either." She wiped her face and watched the little ants rush into different directions.

"Pari, will you ever come out from underneath that damn bush?" Her mother's sharp tone was alarming, but not compelling enough to drag her out from her safe spot.

Somehow she felt safe underneath that barberry bush. By now, she had a special bond with it. Even though each time she crawled underneath it, and was scratched and poked by its thorns, she did not mind it as much. She often picked the barberries when they were bright red and ready to be eaten. She also talked to the bush while picking the berries. Her mother spread them on an old sheet of white cloth and sundried them. She would cook them with rice. They were too sour to be eaten raw.

The barberry bush had grown into an oversized plant with its branches spreading out wildly into different directions. Its unusual size surprised everyone who saw it for the first time. Pari stretched her legs as far as the branches of the bush allowed it. She laid on her back and looked up at the little red berries dangling low, some of them almost touching her face. She started to count the barberries on the branches closest to her. The feel of the soft dirt on her back, the exhaustion from all the crying, and the little berries' hypnotizing stare soon lulled her to sleep.

3

Pari's dream was very vivid. She was standing on an anthill surrounded by little ants, but all of a sudden, each ant grew bigger and bigger. First, their heads grew big, then their bodies. They began to march toward her as their antennae waved back and forth. She wanted to run, but it felt like she had been paralyzed. As the ants began to tower over her, she tried to scream, but her voice was gone. All of a sudden, she saw her mother standing at the bottom of the anthill. She screamed her name incredibly loud. She was beginning to climb the monstrous anthill toward her. She tried to reach out to her. Pari leaned forward to grab her mother's hand. She lost her balance and began falling from the top of the enormous anthill. As she was sliding down, she passed her mother, who was still clinging to the side of the anthill. She looked at Pari with horror and let out a bloodcurdling scream. Pari opened her eyes and realized she was still lying underneath the barberry bush. She felt hot, and the little beads of sweat trickled down her neck. She was relieved. It had just been a bad dream. As she tried to maneuver her body to crawl out from underneath the bush, her mother's desperate screams and sobs stopped her in her tracks. Her heart skipped a beat, her mouth suddenly grew dry, she realized that she might have woken up to her worst nightmare.

4

Pari was always very close to her father. She admired his tall and strong built, his coarse and sometimes unkempt mustache that irritated her skin every time he planted a kiss on her cheek. Her father realized how heartbroken she was when her school was burnt down. He had gone to all the gatherings of the village elders discussing the rebuilding of the school. Ultimately a decision was reached. The rebuilding of the girls' school was going to pose safety threats to everyone in the village. Rumors circulated that the school would be burnt down again, and anyone involved in the process of rebuilding it would be punished. Villagers already lived in fear. Some even believed that girls did not need to be educated; ultimately, they would become wives and mothers. All they needed to learn was how to be an obedient, good wife. Her father did not agree as he always encouraged her to learn. The day her father had come home with the final decision of

17

the village elders, Pari cried herself to sleep. The next day she had woken up by an old storybook by her pillow. The cover was faded and worn out, but the title was bold. As she looked closer, she realized that the last owner had retraced and filled in each letter with black ink. New books were a rarity. People who loved to read tried to preserve them as well as they could, as those books were to be handed down to others. Pari shuffled through the pages with excitement. She lifted the curtain that separated her room from her parents. Her father sat on the mattress as he looked up at Pari with a big smile.

"Well, if you can no longer go to school, grandfather and I will try to find books to bring home for you. It won't be easy, but we will try!"

Pari's father and grandfather were working as land-mine clearing crew. He had told Pari how all this started with Russia invading Afghanistan and the long years of civil war that followed. Pari was too young to understand how dangerous the land-mine removing job was. But on several occasions, when she could not sleep, she had heard her mother cry softly, begging her father to consider finding another job. Every morning as her mother packed food for her father and grandfather, a dark cloud of worries covered her face. Sometimes she mumbled to herself and sobbed as soon as they left for work. There were times when father and grandfather were unusually late returning from work. After pacing up and down the courtyard many times, she wore her burqa and grabbed Pari's hand, dragging her out of the door. In the dusty, narrow alley, Pari could barely keep up with her mother. Her mother took big strides as she panted and breathed heavily. By the end of the alley, they came to a complete stop. Her mother seemed to be focused on the main dirt road. Pari could never tell for sure what her mother looked at from behind the burqa. The mesh screen of the burqa that allowed women to see was very small. It has to be like peeping through tiny keyholes, Pari often wondered. She always dreaded the day she would have to wear the burqa, she was sure she would hate it. As they both stood there watching bicycles, cars, and peddlers go by, Pari focused on the cloud of dust that followed every moving object. Like a lost ghost trying to stalk anything for as long as it could. The dust filled her lungs. She could taste the smoke of the old cars invading her senses mercilessly. This was where her father and grandfather would get dropped off after work by a white, old, and screeching pickup truck. As soon as her mother spotted the truck, she turned around and dragged Pari behind her, but thankfully this time toward their mud house. As always, she told her not to utter a word to her father, as her father did not like her leaving the house unaccompanied by either grandfather or he himself. It was not safe for a woman to roam around freely without being teased, verbally abused, and sometimes questioned.

5

As Pari still lay down underneath the barberry bush, she froze in fear. She had woken up by what seemed to be wailing and screams. She tried to lift up a low hanging branch to get a clear look at what seemed to be a number of people gathered by the door. The dusty yard seemed sad and grey. There was a stretcher with what looked like a lump covered by a white sheet. Pari's hands trembled with fear and her heart raced as she attempted to make sense of all of this. As she was trying to crawl out from underneath the bush, she noticed the bloodstains on the sheet. She saw her mother kneeling down by the stretcher, screaming and beating her chest in agony. Her face and hair were gray, covered with dust. She seemed like a clay figure that was disintegrating and melting in with the soil on the ground. She screamed and sobbed. The neighbors poured into the courtyard one by one, looking down with their hands clasped in front of them.

Pari put her face on the ground and started to cry. She watched her tears make small puddles as her gasps blew the dust into her nose and eyes. She swatted at branches of the barberry bush with anger and broke off as many as she could. The thorns punctured her fingers and tugged at her skin, leaving thin bloodied lines, but she could care less. The pain that she felt inside was much more intolerable. She screamed and kicked as a neighbor finally dragged her out by her legs. As soon as she kicked her ankles free from the neighbor's grip, she crawled to her mother's side, who was now surrounded by women from the neighborhood, consoling her.

That was the last time Pari ever hid underneath the barberry bush. The days and weeks that followed were filled with pain, agony, and tears. Pari later had learned from her grandfather how the mine explosion had claimed her father's life and blown off his leg.

That day, Pari's father and grandfather had eaten their lunch in the shadow of a birch tree. On their way back to work, they had walked the path that was cleared of all the land mines, as the green paint on the rocks along the path indicated a safe route. As they walked towards the truck to pick up their tools, Pari's father was in deep conversation with her grandfather.

"You see *Padar* (father), this land has not had any time to heal. This soil must be tired of soaking up blood. Thousands of people are still killed and maimed every year by these monsters that are hiding underground." Pari's father took a deep breath and wondered out loud.

"How many more would have to die? Every time I deactivate a land mine, I whisper to it. I tell it that you can no longer hide under this dirt, spill blood, and take lives."

Pari listened to the last words of her father narrated by her grandfather. She sobbed softly. She imagined a vast and dry land. There were gaping cracks through which these monsters peeked and preyed on unsuspecting people. They were monsters made out of steel, their eyes made out of fireballs, and claws were sharp and ready to strike. They waited in the dark alleys of the underground, hoping to finally unleash the rage, spew the smoke, rattle the ground and soak up the blood. That day, one of those hideous monsters had found Pari's father.

After weeks of hospital stay, Pari's grandfather was finally brought home. He was no longer the same. He took to his tiny room and barely came out. He struggled to block the memories that haunted him day and night. Too often, he screamed and cried in his sleep. Most nights, Pari stared at the mud ceiling of the room as she laid down on an old mattress next to her mother. She wondered if her mother missed Father as much as she did.

6

Winter was abnormally cold and brutal that year. A thick layer of snow had covered the worn out and cracked sidewalks and streets. The piles of garbage and waste seemed like heaps of disguised monsters dressed in a white blanket of snow. But there was nothing that could disguise the stench that lingered around, like a loyal and faithful servant who never abandoned its master's side. Pari curiously looked around as she walked alongside her mother. As cars drove by, a big splash of mud and slushy snow attacked the pedestrians who, in turn, cursed, spat, and waved fists at the motorists. In spite of the unbearable cold and almost impassable roads, the bazaar buzzed with customers. Usually, on such a day, peddlers placed their carts strategically—the farther the carts from the main road, the better the chances of getting customers. The muddy slush sprayed by the cars angered customers. They jumped up to the side or behind the cart when they heard a car approach. All the items and produce on the carts were carefully covered by a thick sheet of plastic. The peddlers took cover under old umbrellas erected on the back of the carts. They shivered and tried to warm themselves up by sipping hot tea. Men seemed worried. They gathered around carts as they examined and chose the best produce. Some women wearing burqas stood quietly behind their husbands or fathers, while others carefully placed the produce in the plastic bags.

Pari looked up at the dark grey sky above. She followed the dancing snowflakes with her eyes as they landed on her face, nose, and eyelashes. *The wind decides your destiny, beautiful little snowflakes*, she thought. "Some of you might land on the beautiful wool hats, some on the tall rooftops overlooking the alley, and some on the piles of garbage," she exclaimed out loud.

"Pari! Be quiet!" Her mother hissed at her from underneath her burqa. She grabbed her arm, urging her to walk faster. After Pari's father was killed, her mother had taken odd jobs of washing clothes, cleaning homes, and sewing to feed the family. They barely survived every day as the prices of vegetables, flour, oil, and everything else had skyrocketed. That day she was taking Pari along with her to buy more spools of threads and needles for the sewing machine.

"How am I supposed to hurry?" Pari protested as she freed her wrist from her mother's tight grip. "My shoes are too big. They keep coming off my feet. They are getting stuck in the mud and snow! Plus, the soles with all the holes in them are soaking up the water like sponges! My feet are getting numb. I am surprised I can still carry these sinking boats on my feet! I don't know how you can even walk with that thing covering your head to toe. I am struggling with my chador… "But before she could finish, Pari's foot slipped on a patch of ice. As she was falling to the ground, a big gust of wind made her scarf slip off her head. Her mother gasped in fear. Pari's curly black hair fell to her shoulders, and it danced and swayed in the wind mixed with snowflakes. All of a sudden, all the men in the bazaar stopped and glared at her bare head with anger and hatred. Their fierce looks accompanied by curses and lewd remarks angered Pari while she struggled back up to her feet.

"Look at you, shameless sheep with curly fur!" hollered a man cycling past her.

In a panic, Pari's mother frantically covered her head and shoved her thick hair underneath her chador. Pari pushed her hands away in contempt and arranged her scarf with quick moves.

"Hurry up! Let's move fast before you get us stoned or thrown in jail, Pari!" her mother hissed at her with anger.

"It is not my fault. I didn't do it intentionally. Who are these men to chide me for exposing my head?" Pari's voice got louder as her lips quivered with anger mixed with fear. A man with a turban and a shawl wrapped around him took a few steps toward them, looking at them with resentment.

Pari's mother grabbed her arm and began to take fast and wide steps while dragging Pari behind her.

"Quick, Pari!" she begged. Her voice shook with panic.

"Do you see the man coming toward us?" She continued. "Keep your mouth shut and don't argue if we get stopped. Do you hear me?"

Pari turned around and saw the man taking quick steps toward them, angry wide steps as he splashed mud and slush around. By now, a sense of fear and panic crawled through every pore of her body. She held her mother's cold hand with all the strength in her body as she tried to keep up with her.

"Stop!" The man in the black turban commanded.

"Help us, *kohda jan* (dear God), help us please!" Pari's mother prayed softly. They both froze in their tracks.

"How old is your daughter?" The man asked. "How come she is not wearing a burqa?" he demanded.

"Dear brother, she is only eleven years old," responded her mother as she softly pinched Pari's arm.

Pari just stared at her shoes and tried not to make eye contact with the turban-wearing man.

"She looks much older to me." The man retorted with sarcasm. "Maybe it is time to get a burqa." The man glanced at Pari, then quickly looked around at the men who were all listening intently from far away. He cleared his throat and continued, but this time with almost a whisper.

"Go home. Be very careful next time. I have a daughter myself." He continued as he bent down to scrape off the snow on his shoes.

"You might not be able to get away with such a shameful incident next time."

Pari's mother sighed with relief and held on tight to her burqa.

"Thank you. May God keep you and your family safe." Her voice almost inaudible.

Pari's heart sank with pain. She felt full of remorse and regret. Her head hung low and she once again began to walk alongside her mother, only this time her attention was not focused on the holes in her shoes, the dancing snowflakes or the squeaking sound of her shoes soaking up the water from the melting snow. She followed her mother with quick and precise steps, and she did not want to make her upset by lagging behind. They passed a narrow street and all of a sudden, her mother took a sharp turn and entered a dark alley. She looked around with quick moves, and once assured no one was there, she lifted her burqa, grabbing Pari by her shoulders.

"Look at me, Pari! By now you should know when to keep quiet and when to speak up." She looked around cautiously once again before she continued. This time, staring directly into Pari's eyes. "As a woman, you either follow their rules or be ready to face the consequences."

Pari tried to speak up. But her mother placed her hand on her mouth and continued scolding her.

"No more talking back. I'll be devastated if anything happened to you," her voice shook as she fought back the tears. Pari could not bear to look at her mother's fear and grief-stricken face. She turned and looked away. It hurt her so much to see how her mother's beauty had faded away. After her father's death, deep lines covered her forehead. Her cheeks were sunken, her eyes had ceased to sparkle, and a sense of sadness never left her face. In an effort to tune her out, she began to stare into the distance. That is when she noticed a frail dark shadow standing at the opposite side of the alley. All of a sudden, the little shadow began to approach them hesitantly.

"Pari!" Her mother's stern voice startled her.

"Are you even listening to me?" she asked.

Now, the sound of little steps became more audible.

It alarmed Pari's mother. She quickly lowered her burqa and looked into the direction of the sound, expecting to see someone walking toward them. Pari's sudden loud laughter echoed within the walls of the alley.

"Please, Mother! "Pari took her mother's hand between hers, squeezing them with assurance. "Don't be so fearful. It is only a little dog. Perhaps he is hurt, I can tell by the limp." Pari's mother lifted the burqa and squinted her eyes in an effort to focus better. She sighed with relief as she saw the little dog limping toward them.

"How can you even see properly through those little holes? Your eyes probably feel like prisoners who are looking at the world through jail cell windows!" Pari tugged at her mother's burqa and went on to make fun of her.

"Today, you could not tell what was approaching you," Pari burst out laughing. "Perhaps, one day, you will mistake a lion for a cat, and a donkey for a dog." Her mother took one look at Pari and before she could say a word, muffled laughter shook her body. Now much closer, the little dog came to a halt and sat on his hind legs. He looked at Pari and her mother with curiosity, his nose wiggling and his sense of smell worked hard to familiarize himself with the scent of these two strangers. His eyes inquisitive, his fur covered with mud and his little body weak and frail.

He looked at Pari with sadness. There was no shortage of stray dogs in the village. They roamed the streets and alleys, hunting for food. In the summer, they took shelter underneath the shade of the trees, and as they lay there, a swarm of flies and mosquitoes never ceased to pester them. Pari had noticed in the winter, most of them took shelter underneath the wooden platform of the bakery. She had noticed them quite a few times, as little shiny eyes had glared at her numerous times whenever she had passed the bakery. Most of the stray dogs perished in winter as their main source of food, the heaps of garbage alongside the streets and curbs turned into dirty and frozen ice sculptures. They lived at the mercy of strangers who once in a while, threw some leftover food at them. But in a place where people struggled to feed themselves, that was a rarity.

"You poor little thing," Pari whispered and approached the little dog. "You must be so cold and famished. Your paws are covered with snow. They look like ice cubes. Don't worry, look at mine," Pari held up her foot and wiggled her shoe in front of the little dog's face as she continued, "I don't have any fur covering mine. My toes are about to fall off! Now, don't you get excited! You won't get to eat them right away. They need to be thawed out first!" Pari turned around to take a look at her mother and as she caught a glimpse of her mother's furious face, she realized she was in trouble, once again. She quickly slipped her old shoe on and hesitantly followed her mother out of the alley, looking back every now and then at the little white dog who followed her eagerly with his eyes.

7

"But Mother, why can't we take him home," Pari continued to plead as her mother sternly navigated her through the crowded bazaar. "I am sure he will die in this cold."

"Stop it, Pari!" her mother said furiously. "I am not going to listen to this anymore. We can't feed ourselves and barely survive every day. The dog would not be any better off with us. At least here on the streets, he will have the freedom of roaming around in the hope of finding food."

After realizing that her plea was falling on deaf ears, Pari reluctantly kept up with her mother's fast pace. Every now and then, she looked back to see if the limping little grey shadow was following them. But it was difficult to tell since there were numerous mounds of dirty snow lined up against the sidewalk and stores. Pari thought those heaps of snow looked like winter soldiers guarding the streets. But helpless against the brutal dirt and smoke that lingered in the air, they looked defeated and broken. A sudden strong gust of wind took Pari's breath away.

Tired and shivering under the freezing cold, Pari, her voice crackling, told her mother, "Are we almost there?"

The thread store was brightly lit. The bare bulbs hung low from black wires attached to the wooden slat of the ceiling. The wires were crisscrossed and extended to different corners. Pari looked up at the bulbs hanging at the end of those wires. They seemed like glowing spiders descending from a messy web, staring at customers. If one got too close to it, one could feel the heat spewing from them. A wobbly wooden table extended almost throughout the length of the small shop. On it, the colorful spools of thread were arranged neatly. The shop's smell was an unflattering mixture of coal burning in the stove and the soup cooking on top. Pari did not mind the trail of smell following her as she looked at the brightly colored thread spools. *This is much better than walking in the freezing weather outside*, she thought. *I am beginning to feel my toes again.* The shopkeeper was an old man wearing a brown wool hat with folded up trims. His beard was white and sparse, and every time he smiled, he exposed one jagged upper tooth on otherwise bare gums.

He reminded Pari of her grandfather, only Grandfather was so much skinnier. As usual, winter had not been kind to Grandfather's health. His coughing spells had become more frequent, which at times left him gasping for air.

"Here, take this." The shopkeeper's voice startled Pari. She turned around and saw the shopkeeper holding a piece of bread.

"My wife makes the best bread in the neighborhood." He grinned as he continued. "I have some soup here too, you two are welcome to it."

Pari quickly glanced at her mother in search of any signs of approval on her face. But before her mother could say anything, Pari wondered out loud:

"Any meat in the soup?" Before the shopkeeper could answer and to her mother's horror, she went on to ask, "Did you cook it with meat on the bone, or just the vegetables?"

"Pari, what has gotten into you?" Her mother scolded her as she looked apologetically at the shopkeeper. But before she could say another word, the old man laughed heartily.

"Please, don't be upset with her," he said with a reassuring voice. "She sounds exactly like my grandchildren. We can only afford to cook meat on special occasions. Well, maybe that is a good thing for me. I no longer have the teeth to chew anyways." He laughed out loud as Pari's mother still looked embarrassed.

8

Pari thought the walk back home was more treacherous now that the evening was approaching. More puddles and potholes had frozen over. The dirt and pieces of trash trapped underneath the thin sheet of ice seemed eerie. Every now and then, she tried to crack the ice with the tip of her shoe in an attempt to free up whatever was taken hostage by the potholes. The bazaar felt like it had begun to retreat into darkness in an attempt to hide from an unknown evil. The dark grey clouds lingering overhead seemed like angry ghosts ushering people into their homes. Pari's heart was getting heavier and heavier with every step away from the bazaar. The thought of the limping little dog left all alone in the cold and dark alleys made the tears well up in her eyes. She turned around several times and looked back as far as she could manage to see, but the thick curtain of snow distorted her vision each time. She held on tightly to the plastic bag with the spools of thread in it and the piece of bread the old shopkeeper had given her.

"Dogs like bones, not bread," Pari mumbled. "I would have appreciated a bone from the soup much more than the piece of bread."

Pari's mother continued to forge ahead, pretending she did not hear her. She walked in silence in front of Pari. The edges of her burqa were drenched with melting snow and mud. Little pieces of frozen snow stuck tenaciously to the already worn out hems of her burqa. Pari watched intently as every now and then she tried to shake off the pieces of icicles from the garment, but failed to loosen up those icicles stubbornly hanging on. Maybe they are afraid too, Pari wondered. They are escaping from the darkness just like us, she concluded. The steep uphill climb of the narrow alley leading up to the house was much more difficult in winter. It seemed like a battle between the slippery ground and the pedestrian's will. Every step forward was met with resistance as if the snow and the soil had conspired to keep one at a standstill or even worse, pushing back the distance already traveled with much toil. Pari looked up and as far as her vision and the thick white veil of snow could allow her to see, the rooftops of the mud houses were covered by a thick blanket of snow. The outline of the closely built houses reminded Pari of the faces of a crowd of old men and women with silvery grey hair. The thick cracks on the surface of the walls seemed like wrinkles that had invaded those faces.

The little windows resembled sets of gloomy eyes that never blinked while being choked by the smoke coming out of the soot-covered black chimneys.

The loud and desperate creaking of the rusted metal door, planted in the middle of the aged mud wall that surrounded their little house, jolted Pari as she realized they had reached home. As her mother bolted the door shut behind them, Pari squeezed the piece of the bread in the bag tightly.

9

That night Pari was awakened by the distant sounds of gunshots. She quickly sat up on her mattress as she found herself drowned in the utter darkness of the room. The fire in the old wood-burning stove had died down, and the lifeless silver ashes glowed dimly from afar. The mounted pile of ashes seemed like sad ghosts peeking through the thin crisscrossed metal bars of the stove's door, like prisoners taken hostage, Pari thought as her heart raced with fear. The sounds of gunshots got louder, closer, and the interval between each gunshot seemed shorter. Pari never got used to these sounds, even though it occurred frequently. Each time the sounds terrified her as much as the first time she came to hear them, or old enough to realize what they were. She had jumped into her father's arms and had refused to let go until she finally fell asleep. "I miss you, Father," Pari mumbled. She abhorred the terrifying sounds of gunfire immensely.

"Mother," she whispered as her hand searched frantically for her mother's mattress on the floor next to her. "Do you hear this? Are you awake?" She asked with a whisper that unintentionally turned into a thin pitched, loud plea.

"I hear it, Pari," her mother's faceless voice pierced through the blackness of the small room. "Don't be afraid, here hold my hand," she said reassuringly as Pari felt her mother's rough and cracked hand on top of hers.

"Sometimes I think we should be used to the monstrous sounds of explosions and gunfights by now," Pari's mother sighed as she continued,

"This land is cursed, haunted by bloodshed and unrest. Each night these horrific sounds are like dark lullabies that put innocent people to sleep forever… "Pari's mother's voiced quivered as she tried to fight her tears back.

Pari inched closer to her mother and wrapped her arms around her. She blindly kissed her hand in the dark. Pari sensed how withdrawn and resigned her mother had become after her father was killed. Her mother reminded her of a sad little bird in a cage that she had seen in a bird store in the bazaar. As she had passed the store one day, she was astonished by the chaotic mixture of melodies bursting out from the store. Some cages were hung outside, while others were placed on the long wooden tables. The shopkeeper was busy filling the tiny clay cups attached to the bars of the cages with birdseed. There was one little bird that just sat on the horizontal bar that ran across the cage, she sat there silently unaffected by all the noise and chirping that had taken over the store. There was something so sorrowful about it that it saddened Pari. *Maybe she is lonely, maybe she hates being captive, or maybe she has lost someone she loved*, Pari wondered. *Just like Mother*, she concluded.

Grandfather's loud coughs coming from across the narrow and dark corridor pierced through Pari's thoughts. The thunderous sound of the gunfire had subsided. She could feel her mother's peaceful breathing next to her temple. The room was beginning to feel frosty. Pari pulled the patched-up quilt over her head as she remembered the little limping dog. She wondered if it had joined the rest of the stray dogs taking shelter underneath the wooden platform of the bakery. She pictured them all huddled up while their eyes intently followed the hail of bullets exchanged between faceless shadows.

"I know you are afraid, just like the rest of us," Pari whispered, her head still tucked in underneath the quilt.

That night Pari tossed and turned. The cold draft from the window continued to sneak into the room. The thick sheet of plastic covering it flapped every now and then. They could only keep the fire burning for a few hours every night as the cost of wood went up every winter. Now, with Father's income gone, Pari's mother was the sole breadwinner.

Pari slid her hand under her pillow and carefully pulled a book out, the last book that was given to her by her father. She held it close to her chest as she gingerly sat up on her mattress. Next, she folded the edge of her mattress and pulled out a candlestick and a box of matches.

As the little matchstick blew life into the candle, the bright golden halo engulfed Pari's face and her long dark curly hair. She opened her book.

The book's pages were old and yellow. The bottom corners of each page were so worn out that the page numbers were no longer visible. *Probably hundreds of previous owners leafed through them*, Pari thought. Almost every page was smeared with black fingerprints and stains. Pari looked at the fingerprints intently and imagined them as footprints left behind of all those readers who traveled through the book's magical world. The book was missing the last few pages, but that did not stop Pari from reading it over and over again. She imagined herself as the main character in the story and looked at the world through her eyes. At times she fantasized devouring the palatable cuisines that she had never heard of; at other times she enjoyed the brave adventures. The book was like an alluring and beautiful creature with mammoth soft wings. The wings glistened through the night as it navigated through the meadows and mountains with Pari holding tight as she rode this kind creature, who took her away from the four walls of the mud house. Each night she imagined a different ending to the story. That night she imagined landing in the alley where the little limping dog was.

10

Pari was awakened by the familiar sound of her mother's sewing machine. She saw her mother hunched over the old machine. Her face was so close to it that her nose almost touched the twirling thread spool laced through a metal piece on top. Her mother often complained that her vision was getting weaker. She blamed it on all the tears she shed after her father was killed. On one occasion, Pari had convinced her mother to try on grandfather's glasses, but that did not go very well. Grandfather's glasses were missing an arm that was replaced by a long piece of an elastic rubber band that looped around his ear. As soon as Pari was done with putting them on her mother's face, she hurriedly took a few steps and eventually ran into the wall. Instead of rushing to help her, Pari burst out laughing. She laid on her back, laughing hysterically while her mother struggled to take the elastic rubber band off. She cursed Pari and threw a shoe at her for making fun of her, but Pari hid behind Grandfather and continued to giggle.

Later that morning, after Pari emptied the ashes out of the wooden stove, she started to cough relentlessly. Normally, she covered her mouth with her headscarf to avoid inhaling the dust that arose from the ashes. But that morning, she was preoccupied with thoughts. After a good scolding, her mother sent her out to the courtyard to get fresh air. It was no longer snowing, but the sky still looked sullen and grey.

"Hey, Pari!" The voice startled Pari. "What are you doing?" the voice continued. "Here, this way. It's me, Aalia."

Pari looked at the direction of the voice and saw a face peeking from over the wall that separated their house from the neighbors. Every now and then, instead of coming through the door, Aalia made an unexpected entrance from over the wall. This was much more convenient as she did not have to go through the ritual of wearing a burqa and walking in the alley. Instead, all she had to do was climb up the wooden ladder that was always erected horizontally against their side of the wall, and use Pari's ladder to climb down into her courtyard.

"Be careful, Aalia," Pari shouted. "The ladder is slippery. Every step is covered with a thick layer of ice…"But before she could finish, Aalia missed a step and came tumbling down on a big pile of snow.

"Aalia, are you okay?" Pari screamed as she hastily walked toward her. Aalia just lay there motionless, her arms sprawled, fists clenched. Her red quilted coat had a few big holes, through which the white cotton was poking out. Pari sat down next to her and shook her gently.

"Hey, get up…" but before she could say anything else, Aalia suddenly sprang up and smeared a handful of snow in Pari's face. Pari barely had any time to react before Aalia pushed her down in the snow and began to throw fistfuls of snow at her. Between giggles, Pari gathered all her strength as she tried to wiggle out from underneath Aalia. After a few minutes, they both gave up and Aalia just lay on her back next to Pari on the snow-covered ground.

"My hands are frozen stiff," Pari complained as she blew on her hands in an attempt to warm them up. She gazed at the little clouds that escaped her mouth as she exhaled. Against the backdrop of black and dense clouds of the sky overlooking at them, they resembled little ghosts taking off and melting away into the distance.

"Do you believe in ghosts Aalia?" Pari asked wearily.

"Why? Planning to turn into one?" Aalia replied as she lay there next to her, also gazing at the dark sky. "Nowadays, it is much easier to turn into a ghost than to continue to live, especially for girls like you and me," Aalia continued, "Men would have to die first, but in our case, we are already ghosts." Aalia sighed as she sat up.

"You need to do the opposite, Pari. Don't let a burqa turn you into a ghost when you step outside. Don't glide into a sea of faceless ghosts who are only distinguished by the color of their burqas," Aalia stared at Pari sternly as she continued. "Thousands of men have died fighting this never-ending war, but women have been buried alive within the four walls of their homes, deprived of the most basic rights and education."

Aalia was nineteen, but she appeared much younger due to her short stature. She had a round face and the short brown hair framed her face perfectly. A thick scar ran across her left forehead and cheek. At nineteen, she was already married and divorced. Her husband was convinced that she was barren as she failed to give him a child after four years of marriage. Aalia often joked about her scar and referred to it as the only trace of her marriage that she could not erase. She often talked to Pari as how delighted she was to be divorced and free from the clutches of her abusive husband. Aalia never attended school and she always expressed her frustration and bitterness about being illiterate. Pari sensed that she had struck a nerve. She quickly sat up and began to brush the snow off of her sleeves and back. She glanced at the snow-covered little courtyard and the sight of the unusually tall barberry bush made her heart skip a beat. The shrub seemed like an old woman wearing a white cloak, with arms protruding at each side. Aalia's angry voice faded in the background as Pari could hear her heart pulsate rapidly. She resented that barberry bush and had vowed never to shelter underneath it. It was always a harrowing reminder of the day her father was killed.

"Aalia, do you think my father can see me?" Pari asked almost in a whisper, her voice shaking.

Aalia looked surprised by Pari's question as she struggled to come up with an answer. She looked at Pari and followed the direction of the object that Pari's eyes were transfixed on. *The damn barberry bush*, Aalia thought. Pari had recounted the incident to Aalia many times.

"Look at me, Pari," Aalia said as she cupped Pari's cold face between her equally frosty hands. "You know that you are dear to me and I love you like a little sister. Your father will always live in your heart." She kissed Pari on the forehead. "It is time that you forgave that barberry bush. Don't let fear intimidate you. I know you are strong, Pari."

"Pari," her mother interrupted them. "You need to light the fire in the stove."

Aalia stood up and extended her hand to help Pari up. "I don't know about you, but my butt is frozen." Aalia chuckled.

"Aalia, once I am done lighting the stove, can you please tell me that ghost story again?" Pari begged Aalia.

"No, not today, Pari," Aalia said. "I need to get back home. I just came over to check up on you."

"Please, please, Aalia. I beg you." Pari insisted. Aalia looked at Pari and frowned.

"Only on one condition," Aalia agreed as she continued. "You will have to read me a few pages from your storybook, and this time I get to decide how it ends." Pari eagerly shook her head in agreement.

After the fire was lit and the red flames began to dance inside the little stove, Pari, her mother, and Grandfather huddled together right next to it. Aalia cleared her throat and began the story.

Once upon a time in a far, far, away land, there used to be a ghost who lived in the wall of a house facing the street. He was tall, oval, and white as snow. His eyelashes were made out of long strands of sparkling crystals and his eyes were green as grass. He loved to scare the passersby every day as they went about their daily lives. He relished his power of frightening people and laughed each time someone was terrified. The ghost jumped out of the wall in front of unsuspecting walkers and screamed "Boo" each time. Some screamed in fear, some took off running, never looking back, and some simply rubbed their eyes in disbelief. After years of living in the same wall, he got restless and his routine felt monotonous and dull. He decided to travel and relocate to a new and exciting place and to find an interesting wall to live in. After months of traveling, he reached a village in Afghanistan. He decided to spend some time there and see if it was to his liking. He liked the tall mud walls that surrounded the village. He wondered about the little holes that covered the wall in different places. He thought maybe they were intricate designs that were placed skillfully into the grooves of the wall. But on the very first night, he expeditiously discovered that he was wrong. He shifted from one section to another section as random bullets kept on piercing the wall. *I hate this*, he thought to himself, *but I will have plenty of fun terrifying people tomorrow.* The next day as the sun was getting ready to retire behind the tall mountains and the sun cast an orange shadow on the ground, the ghost took position and grinned in anticipation of shocking and frightening people. He noticed an old man walking with a wooden stick, lost in deep thoughts. The ghost sprang in front of him with a loud thud, and yelled, "Boo!" The old man kept on walking with his head hung low, unbothered. The ghost was surprised. He had never failed to scare anyone before. Maybe he was deaf and slightly blind, he consoled himself. He waited patiently as he kept himself entertained by counting the bullet holes in the wall, and every now and then poking his fingers in them. He took position as he heard some footsteps approaching the wall. This time he sprang out of the wall with his arms up in the air while making a terribly loud and ear-piercing sound. All three passersby continued to walk on unaffected by it all. The ghost was absolutely shattered. He concluded that he had lost his power and had become totally invisible. He sat there on the dusty ground and he held his head between his hands. He began to sob quietly. The sound of laughter from a distance jolted him. He looked in the direction of the sound and saw a little boy sitting underneath a tree and looking right at him. He is looking at me, the ghost thought, maybe I have not become invisible after all. He got up and walked toward the little boy. The little boy continued to sit there, unafraid and calm as he approached him soundlessly.

"Do you see me?" Asked the ghost impatiently.

"Yes, I can, and I am not afraid of you." Replied the little boy trying to sound tough.

"How come no one else can see me?" The ghost asked his voice filled with curiosity and wonder. "No one is shocked or terrified of seeing me? I have never failed to scare people, yet no one seems to be even bothered by me."

"You have not been to my village before," the little boy said as he continued. "We have been through a lot of hardships and wars. It is not ghosts we fear. We are afraid of living people who are evil. We are afraid of bombs, guns, land mines, and hunger." The little boy stopped and stared at the ghost. The ghost looked down to avoid his stare. He felt sad for him.

"By the way," the little boy whispered quietly. "Why do you think it is fun to scare people? Being afraid is not a good feeling. When I am afraid my heart beats really, really fast and my throat feels like it closes up," the little boy explained wearily.

The ghost just sat there thinking, pondering and very embarrassed.

"So, what is your name and why are you sitting here?" asked the ghost looking at the little boy inquisitively.

"My name is Arman. It means wish. I come here and sit under this apple tree if the night before is filled with loud explosions and gunfights. It is peaceful here." he said, sounding resigned. The ghost looked at the little boy with affection. *He seems so hopeless*, he thought.

"Do you want an apple?" the ghost asked, looking up at the yellow apples hanging high.

"Sure. I tried to pluck one, but the branches are too high for me," he explained bashfully. The ghost glided up and picked a perfect apple from the tree and handed it to the little boy. He was enthralled by the happiness and smile his act of kindness had accomplished.

"By the way, why do you relish scaring people so much?" the little boy asked again as he sank his teeth into the sweet juicy apple. The ghost scratched his head and fell into deep thought. He had never contemplated that. Maybe because no one had ever asked him that before, or maybe because he thought that is just what ghosts did.

"Kindness is better than scaring people," the little boy looked at the ghost and smiled. "My grandfather says if humans understood the true value of kindness and accepting each other, this world would be a better place." The little boy then got up and wrapped his arms around the ghost. The ghost was amazed at how that hug felt so much better than frightening everyone. The little boy bade him farewell and disappeared into the distance. A thin cloud of dust followed him as he walked farther and farther. The ghost decided that he would dwell in the apple tree from that day onwards. All the children in the village came to be enamored with the apple tree that magically dropped an apple every time they took shelter in its cool shade. Everyone in the village offered an explanation, but only Arman knew the truth.

11

That night, as Aalia climbed back down the ladder into her own courtyard, she felt restless. She tried to block the memories that were trying to rush back into her head. Trying to suppress those memories were futile at times. It felt like keeping a monster locked down in the gloomy abyss of her consciousness. But every now and then, that dark beast raised its ugly head, sending her into a free fall into that lightless place.

Aalia took small steps toward her house. There was a dim light coming from a small window outlined by a green wooden frame. Aalia peeked inside the only room of the house that was lit by a kerosene lantern. The sounds of giggling and blabbering coming from the inside made Aalia smile as she stood outside in the cold dark courtyard. She pressed her forehead on the window, her eyes keenly followed a little girl running around the room, sometimes overtaken by bursts of giggles. She was almost two years old, with a perfectly round face and light brown hair. The little girl was dressed in an old oversized sweater that almost looked like a dress on her small frame. She seemed to be fascinated by her gigantic shadow cast on the mud wall of the room. The lantern flickered gently with each burst of excited laughter as if it was taking part in the game of casting shadows on the wall with the little girl. Aalia wrapped her headscarf tighter around her head in an attempt to keep the frigid air out. She rubbed her hands together and tucked them into her old coat's pockets. It was not too long ago that she was sitting in that same room, dressed as a bride. As Aalia continued to peek through the window, those memories slowly slithered back into her consciousness. It felt they were like dark beasts hiding out in the dark alleys of her existence, and every now and then, something unleashed them on her. She tried to keep them at bay, but the longer she looked at the room, the more of those beasts crawled out, and finally, all those memories poured into that room. She saw herself sitting on a red mattress, dressed in a beautiful green dress with intricate gold embroidery. Her palms and the tips of her fingers were covered by red henna. The women were singing and clapping, and at times they just sounded awful, like clacking chickens flapping their wings.

Aalia was blissfully unaware that her life was about to change. That night she devoured the fancy sweets she rarely ate. There was plenty of rice and even meat that went around endlessly. The men congregated outside, smoking hookah and laughing loudly. Aalia's mother seemed sad and refused to eat dinner when offered. She tried to explain certain things to Aalia in the weeks leading to the wedding. But none of what she said had made much sense to her. She remembered asking her mother for only one significant item the week prior to the wedding. Her mother agreed while hugging her tight and sobbing. On the day of the wedding, Aalia pulled out the little doll from underneath her skirt and smiled happily as her outfit matched hers perfectly. Her mother had fulfilled her promise.

The creaking of the door alarmed Aalia, who was still staring into the room with her forehead pressed against the cold window.

"Aalia, how long have you been standing there for?" Aalia's mother asked, sounding surprised. "I have to warm the soup for dinner. Go inside and look after your daughter," she said as she walked off in the dark toward the storage room.

Aalia had kept a secret from everyone who knew her, even her close friend Pari. The month before she was divorced, she had discovered that she was with a child. She knew if her abusive husband found out that she was carrying his child, he would no longer proceed with the divorce. She would have no longer been barren. After returning home, she spent the rest of the pregnancy in the seclusion of her house. Her mother had made the midwife swear to secrecy as Aalia screamed in pain. When the old midwife placed her daughter in her arms, Aalia panicked. The baby was not much bigger than her plastic doll, but she looked at her with awe as her little head rested on her chest. It was love at first sight. She held her close to her body as her hands trembled with relief.

"*Afsana* (fable/story)," Aalia mumbled as she softly kissed her forehead. "I will call you Afsana, and you will be the writer of your own fable, my love."

Aalia looked up and saw her mother weeping soundlessly. She wiped her tears with her headscarf and whispered softly, "I hope you forgive me, my daughter. Someone has to break this vicious cycle. Unfortunately, I was not the strong one. Before we even get to truly know ourselves, our fate is decided." She paused and caressed Afsana's hair. She took an evil eye bead out and pinned it to her swaddle cloth.

"May your story be a happy one, my little angel." She wished as she showered her tiny feet with kisses.

12

Winter was relentless, grandfather thought. He had never seen a winter like this in his long life. It showed no mercy as the frigid air blew day and night. The persistent grey clouds seemed determined to keep the sun at bay during the day and make the nights even gloomier by covering the moon almost every night. He began to sleep in the same room as Pari and her mother during the winter months. There was only one wood-burning stove in the living room that served as a bedroom at night. Pari was feeling anxious as she cautiously observed that their daily food portions were shrinking in volume, and the wood in the stove burned for shorter periods of time. What distressed her the most was when grandfather's coughing spells got worse, or when he moaned in pain in his sleep. One night Pari could not fall asleep. She stared at the mud ceiling as she remembered the days she went to school. At nights she did homework in the light of a kerosene lamp while her father watched her proudly. She missed her father so terribly. She got up and tiptoed to the small window and looked out. That night the moon was hidden under a thick layer of clouds, but every now and then, a narrow stream of light somehow managed to escape illuminating the otherwise pitch-black sky. "Are you playing hide and seek with me?" Pari whispered at the moon softly. "You don't need to try that hard, you are not that difficult to find even if you tried, but I feel like no one can see me even if they tried."

"Pari, come here, dear." Grandfather's voice startled her. She did not realize he was still awake. She carefully crossed the room in the dark and sat down on the floor next to his mattress.

"We will survive this winter, too, God willing. Don't worry." He reassured her as he patted her on the head. "Remember, once I showed you a cocoon when you were very young?" and before Pari could reply, he continued. "Just imagine this winter, we are all wrapped up in a thick fluffy white cocoon of snow, and when the spring comes, we will all emerge as beautiful butterflies." He whispered. "We will fly out in the meadows, sit on flowers, and soak up the sun. That thought makes my old bones feel warmer." He laughed quietly.

"You would look more like a praying mantis," Pari said teasingly. "Always perched up on your prayer rug," Grandfather giggled softly.

"Only, it seems like either God has forgotten about this praying mantis, or He has given up on us altogether." His resigned tone of voice saddened Pari. She did not intend to make him sad. She bent down and hugged him.

"You are the most beautiful praying mantis in the world, Grandfather, even more beautiful than any butterfly," Pari muttered as she put her head on his chest.

That morning Grandfather's loud scream followed by a big thud. It frightened Pari. She was cleaning the ashes out of the stove to light a fire, as she did every morning. She threw the dustpan and broom down. She ran out of the room to the courtyard. She gasped in fear when she noticed Grandfather face down in a pile of snow. Her mother also was running toward him from the opposite side of the courtyard.

"Are you hurt? Did you slip?" Pari asked while kneeling down beside her grandfather. Her mother prayed softly under her breath as she turned him on his back.

"The ground is frozen and slippery," she said in a worried voice. "You should have waited for Pari to help you."

"I am fine," Grandfather said reassuringly as he tried to force a smile. "I don't think I have broken any of my old bones. I think one of my crutches got stuck in the snow and that made me lose my balance." He seemed embarrassed and helpless. Seeing him like that made Pari's heart ache.

"Look at you, Grandfather," Pari said, teasing as she picked up one of his crutches. "You have turned into a snowman! Your beard and head are covered in snow. Let me help you up before you turn into an ice sculpture," she said as she picked up one of his crutches.

"I feel like I am frozen in time, stuck in a place where the sun never shines," he mumbled softly. Pari's mother said another prayer as she got ready to help him off the ground. As Pari picked up the second crutch, she gasped loudly. The lower half of the wooden crutch was broken. She did not know how to tell her grandfather. After all, these were his legs, and without those, he could not move around.

She knew they did not have the money to buy a new one. She just stood there with her back to her mother and grandfather. She did not have the courage to break the news to him.

"Pari, hurry up," her mother's voice distressed her even further, but she just stood there, motionless, "Why are you just standing there?"

"What is it, Pari?" Grandfather's question surprised her. "Is it broken?" She slowly turned around as she held the two broken pieces up. The look on grandfather's face was of disappointment and grief. He sighed and looked at Pari with love.

"Well, let's look at it this way," he tried to sound cheerful but Pari could sense the pain and hurt in his voice. "That could have been my only surviving leg.

A broken crutch is better than a broken leg." She felt the lump in her throat get bigger and her eyes started to sting as the tears welled up. She quickly wiped her eyes and got under her grandfather's arm.

"Well, now you have a human crutch!" Pari said with a chuckle on her face, "All you have to do is call my name and The Pari Crutch will magically appear underneath your armpit." He kissed the top of her head as he slowly hopped to the house with the help of Pari and her mother.

Later that morning, Pari 's mind was wrestling with many ideas of how to get her grandfather's crutch fixed, and each time she ended up at the same conclusion, going to the welder's shop in the bazaar. Perhaps the welder can do a better job than the carpenter, she thought although her mother had already made it clear to her that she was not permitted to go to the bazaar alone. Taliban still had the majority of the village under their control, and the constant war between the government forces and the insurgents did little to clear them away. Pari resented them and blamed them for all the misery they had to face on a daily basis. She sat on the ground with her chin resting on her knees, deep in thought. After some time, she sprang up to her feet, brushed the snow off of her clothes and smiled. She had a plan. She tiptoed to the house and quietly snatched her mother's burqa hanging from a nail dug in the wall. Next, she grabbed two plastic bags and her shoes. Once out of the mud house, she sat on the ground and wrapped the plastic bags around her feet before putting her shoes on. She could still feel the cold snow through the holes in the bottom of her shoes, but the plastic bags prevented the water from seeping through the holes.

13

Pari's mother sat behind the sewing machine, preoccupied with worries that never left her alone. *After I get paid for these*, she thought, *I can have the crutch repaired and buy some sugar and flour.* Her arm ached with the repetitive motion of spinning the sewing machine, but she did not stop. She never heard when the outside gate creaked open and Pari slipped out into the alley.

Fresh snow had fallen the previous night and covered the layer of ice below it. Pari struggled with positioning the small opening of the burqa over her eyes. It gradually slipped lower and lower, covering her vision completely. She had never worn a burqa before. Enveloped in that long garment, it almost suffocated her and restricted her movement. The friction between her shoes and the plastic bags worn as socks made a squeaking sound each time she took a step. Holding tight onto the broken crutch and reaching halfway down the alley, Pari heard a little sound. Hoping to see that little limping dog again, she came to a complete halt and listened carefully. The sound stopped as she looked back and she walked on. Looking through the small opening of the burqa, everything seemed distorted. Walking in a stifling bubble, she felt like she was totally detached from her surroundings. The walk to the bazaar was long. She was already exhausted and labored over every step that she took.

Tired of being handicapped by the unyielding burqa, Pari took it off and tucked it under her arm. She navigated the crowd in the bazaar with caution. She tried not to attract any attention as she walked alongside or behind women with children in tow. She finally found the little dark welding shop in the corner of the main bazaar. The shop was very small with a wooden table and some tools hanging from the walls. The old welder was sitting on a little worn-out mat on the floor. He was drinking tea from a tin cup, making loud intermittent slurping sounds. He had a kind face and reminded Pari of her grandfather.

"*Salaam*," Pari greeted him as she approached him with small steps.

"*Salaam* little one," he looked at Pari. His eyes shifted to the broken crutch Pari was holding. "What can I do for you?" He asked, already guessing the answer. Pari felt relieved. *He seems kind, and hopefully he will not ask for too much money*, she thought.

Pari handed him the two broken pieces and proceeded to tell him all about Grandfather's unfortunate fall that morning. The old welder listened patiently while sipping his tea.

"Well, as you can see, I am not a carpenter. How do you expect me to repair this?" he asked, looking at Pari with curiosity.

"If I take it to a carpenter, it will break again from the same spot. But if you use metal pieces to join them back together, this crutch will last longer," Pari said, sounding determined to change the welder's mind. The old welder smiled as he got up.

"Your grandfather is lucky to have you," he said, "I will see what I can do."

Pari stood in the corner of the shop as the old welder began working on the crutch. As soon as he turned his welding torch on, the flying sparks took over the little dark shop. The flames surrounded the old welder's face in a bluish halo, and his white beard seemed silvery in contrast to the blue light. Pari stepped back every time a spark flew in her direction. They reminded her of the flying bullets in the darkness of the night. Some sparks were stubborn enough to reach her and some just lost their luster halfway in the air, startling her nonetheless.

Pari felt relieved as soon the torch was turned off. The welder proudly handed Pari the mended crutch. Two shining pieces of metal held the wooden pieces together. Pari's heart beat with excitement, but she felt awfully nervous at the same time. It was time to pay the old welder and she was reluctant as she was not going to pay him with money. She felt guilty for not disclosing that right in the beginning, but she was afraid the welder would decline to repair the crutch. She took a deep breath in an effort to gather some courage. She slowly slipped her hand in her coat pocket and took a step forward toward the welder and while trying to avoid looking at him, put a small, round silver earring on the old wooden table.

"Sorry, but I don't have any money to pay you with," she said. Almost, in a whisper, she continued, "But this is silver, it was a gift from my father. You can have this one and I will hold on to the second one. The other crutch is getting very old too, once that needs to be repaired, I will give you the other one. That way you can have a complete pair." Pari stood there with her head hung low, unsure of the old welder's reaction. She was too nervous to even glance at him. *God please help me*, she thought. *Make him accept it*, she prayed. All of a sudden, she felt the rough hand of the old welder grabbing hers, and she felt a round cold piece of metal placed in the palm of her hand. She looked at it with disbelief. The silver earring was back in her hand.

"You and I live in a country of broken dreams, broken futures, and broken people. Here everything is broken...." His voice trailed off and Pari looked up at him. He quickly looked away. "I enjoy putting broken things together. I know the rest will stay broken," he concluded with a frown on his face. "Now, you better run home before you get yourself in a lot of trouble."

It was past midday and Pari began to take hurried steps towards home as she held on tight to grandfather's mended crutch. She attempted to stay focused, but the chaos in the bazaar was too distracting. The various street vendors sold fried fish, potato fritters, and boiled eggs. Pari inhaled the aromas as deeply as she could. She wanted to form a backlog of those enticing smells in her memory and recall it every time she craved something delicious. The golden-colored corn on the cob was being roasted on the small portable stoves while a crowd of poor children surrounded them. Some of those kids were day laborers who were momentarily sidetracked by the aroma. Some others were simply trying to warm up their little bodies with the heat being generated by the black coal stoves.

Pari reached the strip of the spice stores. The myriads of colors displayed were astonishing. The burlap sacks were lined up uniformly, each filled with salt, red pepper, turmeric, cumin, black pepper, and Saffron. Her feet began to sting as shreds of ice stubbornly poked holes through the plastic bags wrapped around her feet. When she squatted down to brush the snow off of her shoes, she noticed the little eyes looking at her from underneath the spice store's wooden platform. The little limping dog was curled up and visibly shaking in the cold. Pari quickly looked around and every few seconds when no one was looking, she moved closer and closer to the little dog. She wanted to grab the little dog without scaring it away. Suddenly, all changed.

A deafening sound of an explosion invaded the surroundings. The ground shook vehemently. The instant smell of smoke and gunpowder violated her senses. Pari remembered seeing a plume of smoke and flames lurching towards her, but by then, she could no longer hear, and if that flaming monster was roaring, Pari was happy she could not hear it. *You cannot catch me*, Pari thought as she tried to hold onto the ground that was quickly slipping from underneath her. People were running, some stepped on her while others tripped and fell. Pari tried to stay alert, she struggled to keep her eyes open, but it felt like a dark, heavy blanket was gradually pulled over her senses. She felt the burning pain but could not distinguish which part of her body was throbbing. Her eyelids got heavier. She choked on the smoke. She moved her arm in an attempt to locate Grandfather's crutch. "No, I am not going to fall asleep," she whispered, but a dark, savage monster was killing all her senses one by one. The screams and loud noises began to fade in the distance as Pari struggled to stay alert. Her many attempts to get up were overpowered by some massive force that kept her pinned down to the ground. As she drifted into a state of unconsciousness, it felt as if she was walking through a long dark tunnel with no end in sight. It was cold and she was walking alone. Voices echoed in the tunnel, but she was not able to see any faces. She heard her mother calling her name. She heard Aaila's voice echoing in the tunnel over and over again, "Are you planning to turn into a ghost?" She heard footsteps and looked back, but there was nothing but darkness. She hurried towards a small yellow spot that appeared suddenly in the distance. She hoped it was the rays of the sun that would guide her out of the darkness. She took off running until the yellow spot got closer. At that moment, she felt something warm on her forehead. She slowly opened her eyes.

There were two little eyes staring back at her. His little tongue licked her forehead one more time. As she lay there, she was terrified to look around as the commotion and screams were becoming gradually audible again. She looked at the little dog that was sitting right next to her. When her eyes could focus better, she realized he was completely covered by a bright yellow spice powder. She gathered all her strength as she sat up on the sidewalk. She hesitantly looked back and froze with fear.

A monstrous fire was burning in the middle of the bazaar. Soldiers were screaming and firing shots. She could not tell if the screams were louder or the gunshots. She quickly looked away and struggled up to her feet. As soon as she was able to stand up, she grabbed Grandfather's crutch and quickly scooped up the little dog. She wrapped him up in her mother's burqa and ran away. Something warm trickled down her face and she felt light-headed and nauseated. She did not want to pass out again, so she made an effort to block the chaos behind her and focus on the little dog. He just nestled quietly in her arms, shaking every now and then. *You must be in shock too*, Pari thought. She tried to run as fast she could, but the frozen ground worked against her, and she slipped and tripped numerous times.

Once she was far enough and the terrifying sounds faded substantially, she leaned against the wall in an alleyway and gasped for air. The alleyway was almost deserted. With the sound of each explosion, frightened people took to their homes, locked the doors, and huddled together. Pari slid down against the wall and sat on the ground, on a pile of dirty snow. She put the little dog, still wrapped up in her mother's burqa, next to her. His little yellow head popped out from underneath the burqa and curiously looked at Pari.

"You don't like the burqa either, right?" Pari patted his spice covered head as she tried to shake off some of the yellow powder from his fur. He took a step forward and began to lick her hand. Pari smiled and rested her head against the wall. The throbbing pain in her head was now even more pronounced. She realized she needed to get up and hurry home, but the bottom of her right foot was burning intensely. Her foot felt numb and heavy. She looked down and noticed that her foot was bare and the shoe was missing. The plastic bag she had tied around her foot was torn and shredded.

With all the fear and panic that seized her body and mind, Pari had not noticed her shoe was left behind. Pari's heart sank. That was the only pair of shoes she owned. The loud sound of a machine gun startled Pari and she quickly got to her feet. Her heart began to pound and her hands began to tremble. She hurriedly scooped up the little dog and began to run. "We need to run before they get to us!" Pari cried out loud as she took off running and limping at the same time.

Earlier, Pari had noticed armored vehicles and soldiers in the bazaar, some riding in the trucks and some on foot. That was not unusual as every time there was a surge in violence, government and foreign soldiers patrolled more often and in greater numbers.

The sound of machine guns began to get closer and echoed between the worn-out mud walls of the alley. With each shot, Pari let out a scream and hugged the little dog tighter. She could feel his fast heartbeat against her own chest.

"Don't be afraid," Pari shouted. "I will get you home safely! I am going to name you Saffron since you are so golden yellow! "She did not know why she was shouting her words, but she could not help it. Maybe she wanted to drown out the sounds of the machine guns, or maybe the hard and fast heartbeats of the little dog combined with hers were terrifying her even more. She ran as she dragged her grandfather's crutch on the snow and ice, leaving an even line behind. Pari heard footsteps of someone running right behind her. She heard men screaming and swearing as they fired more shots. She could see the rusted blue door of her house at the end of the alley, but it seemed too far as she tried to forge forward with every last bit of willpower still left in her body. She felt like the dark shadows of those men were closing in on her, and as a bullet whizzed by her ear, her knees went weak. She noticed a deep ditch by the wall. Without looking back, she dove in it, holding Saffron tight and still wrapped up in the burqa.

14

Pari curled up in a fetal position inside the snow-filled ditch. Saffron began to whimper and squirm around inside the burqa. Pari rubbed his little head in an attempt to quiet him down. She remembered what her father always whispered to her when the sounds of explosions terrorized her.

"This will be over soon, and don't forget there are many guardian angels watching over you," Pari whispered it to Saffron as the footsteps of people running in the alley got closer. She closed her eyes and hugged Saffron tighter. The sounds were now a mixture of clattering footsteps, thunderous voices giving orders, some in a language that Pari could not understand. It felt like the passage of time had come to a crawling pace as Pari tried hard to hold her breath and keep her eyes closed. As the trail of chaos began to dwindle, Saffron, overcome by terror, finally let out a bark. Pari's heart skipped a beat and she froze in fear. She clenched her fists and began to tremble.

Pari heard heavy footsteps approaching the deep ditch. The grating sounds of the leather against the snow frightened her as she attempted to keep her eyes shut. She had heard of punishments that befell girls who were found wandering alone. Panicking, she pushed her hair underneath her chador, her eyes still shut. The eerie sounds of footsteps came to a halt by the edge of the ditch that Pari was hiding in. Pari struggled not to open her eyes. Maybe she wanted to shut out the beast that was lurking at the edge of the ditch. *If I pretend I am dead and lay motionless, he will go away*, Pari thought. The water from the cold snow seeping through her old sweater combined with fear made it impossible for Pari not to move. Her whole body began to quiver.

"Are you hurt?" A woman's voice was not what Pari expected to hear. The sentence was broken, with a strange accent that was unfamiliar. Before Pari opened her eyes, Saffron barked and wiggled out from underneath the burqa. Pari hesitantly opened her eyes. Right above her, crouching over the ditch and looking down at her was a soldier. She was wearing the same uniform she had observed foreign soldiers wear. Her helmet came down to her eyebrows. Pari instantly noticed she had beautiful emerald green eyes, *just like my mother,* Pari thought as she stared at her with awe.

"Hurry up!" The soldier urged as she extended her arm towards Pari. Her urgent and stern tone of voice made Pari hastily sit up, and still in disbelief, quickly grabbed the woman's hand. As soon as she was hoisted up from the ditch, Pari grabbed Saffron and Grandfather's crutch and took off running towards the blue, rusted door. The heavy sounds of the soldier's boots behind her made her feel safe somehow. All of a sudden, that sound created a barrier between her and the danger chasing her. By the time they reached the door to her house, a rain of bullets descended upon them. Pari swiftly pushed the door open and gestured to the solider to run in. Once safely inside, Pari wrapped up a rusty chain around the door handles and with a swift click, she locked the heavy padlock hanging from the old chain. She rested her forehead against the ribbed, metal door and took a deep breath. Loud gasps and the sound of slapping one's forehead made her immediately turn around. She saw three faces staring at her and the soldier, like people frozen in time. Aalia, mother and Grandfather were standing there, looking shocked. Their statuesque glare made Pari realize that she was in bigger trouble than she realized. Saffron hid behind her legs, whimpering softly.

The sudden crackling noises coming from something that seemed like a small speaker jolted all of them. The soldier took a few steps away from everyone and spoke to that piece that was strapped securely to her upper arm. None of the words made any sense to Pari, but she assumed her fellow soldiers were inquiring about her whereabouts. Pari felt deeply guilty and blamed herself for causing her to fall behind. *She stopped to help me*, Pari thought.

"Where have you been, Pari?" her mother finally spoke as she shifted her gaze from the soldier to her. "We have been worried sick, we heard the explosion and now, the chaos that has erupted just outside these walls." Her voice trailed off as she fought the tears back.

"I came looking for you, halfway there I heard the sound of the explosion and I had to run back home," Aalia looked at Pari with anger. "Do you even realize what you have put us through Pari?" Aalia continued, her voice sounding angrier and angrier. Pari's head hung low as she stared at her cold and numb foot, which had become bare except for some pieces of plastic still clinging to her toes.

"You are going to get us all killed Pari," Pari's mother moaned with despair. "Do you know what the insurgents do to people who help foreigners?"

Pari gasped with disappointment and quickly looked at the soldier, who was looking at everyone suspiciously by now. *Hopefully, she did not hear what my mother just said,* Pari wished, looking embarrassed.

"It couldn't be any worse than what they would do to me for not wearing a burqa, or wanting to go to school!" Pari retorted loudly. "She saved my life, and I am not going to let her go back into that back alley infested with bloodthirsty insurgents!" she shouted all of it at once and without taking a breath.

"That is enough!" Grandfather's roaring voice startled Pari. "Afghans don't feed their guests to the wolves! I would rather get killed, knowing that I upheld my values than to go to my grave wearing a veil of shame!" He looked at Pari's mother, angrily. The soldier lifted her gun and shifted from one leg to another, looking apprehensive. All of a sudden, Pari was filled with relief and felt so proud of her grandfather. This was the first time after her father was killed that Grandfather looked so strong, so full of conviction and a voice so strong that it took Pari by surprise. If it was not for his frail body and leaning helplessly on a crutch, one would have thought of him as a tenacious man. With everything that was transpiring, Pari had forgotten to give the mended crutch to Grandfather. She picked up the crutch and threw herself in Grandfather's arms.

"Here, I got it fixed!" and with that, Pari lifted up the crutch and gently placed it under his arm.

"And this is why you went to the bazaar?" Grandfather kissed the top of her head as tears welled up in his eyes.

A sudden thunderous banging on the door and loud voices on the other side of the wall alarmed everyone. The soldier swiftly pointed her gun toward the door. Aaila covered her mouth as a small scream escaped it, her eyes widened in shock. Pari's mother slumped on the ground as if her knees gave in.

"Open this damn door!" A man's voice pierced through the thick layer of fear that seemed to have incapacitated everyone momentarily. Pari's grandfather looked at everyone and put his index finger on his lips. He then soundlessly walked towards the mud wall. It was getting dark, and in the dimming light of the day and snow-covered ground, he seemed like a skinny, floating snowman with thin arms and wooden legs, Pari thought as fear took over her body.

Once by the wall, Pari's grandfather very cautiously took a small brick out of the wall and peeked through the hole. He could see the alley, he squinted to focus better and that is when he saw the shadowy movement of some men standing on the other side of the wall.

15

"You need to hide now!" Grandfather commanded in a whisper. "Aalia, take them to the tandoor room now!" The sense of urgency combined with fear and panic made Pari grab the soldier's sleeve and led her toward the little dark room.

"Hurry, we need to go!" she urged her. "Enemy coming," she attempted to explain to her in simpler words. "Please, come!" she begged as they all tried to run as soundlessly as possible. Once they all got into the tiny mudroom, they took shelter behind a heap of chopped wood piled up high. The room was cold, dark, and humid. The tandoor's (clay oven) round opening always reminded Pari of a gaping mouth that swallowed balls of rolled-up dough and spat out baked bread. The lingering aroma of baked bread mixed with the smell of wood comforted Pari. It took a while until their eyes adjusted to the utter darkness that covered that room. The soldier got on her knees and positioned her weapon in a way that it faced the opening of the little room. She took a deep breath and waited, aiming at the small entrance that let the cold air outside flow in.

Pari could hear the squeaking of the door as Grandfather opened it. She huddled with Aalia and her mother as she began to pray hard. Pari listened intently, worried about Grandfather's safety.

A man's voice was audible as he questioned Grandfather.

"Who lives here with you?" asked the man.

"I live here with my son's widow and my granddaughter," his voice sounding assertive. "We are poor people. We hardly get by every day and have nothing to do with politics or supporting anyone…"

Another man's voice interrupted him. "Aren't you the land mine sniffing dog? Is that how you lost your leg?" he yelled mockingly as a burst of laugher broke out. Pari's mother squeezed her hand hard as she began to sob with fear.

"Are you helping foreigners?" A third man's voice sounded threatening.

"Did a soldier come in here?"

"No, no one came here," Grandfather pleaded, "please leave us alone. Look at me. I can't even take care of myself. We are already half-dead, the rest of this cold winter and hunger will probably put us out of our misery soon," he sounded resigned when he added. "Why have our blood on your hands?"

"We are going to search every inch of this house," the voice said with a menacing tone. "Begin praying that we don't find anyone old man! Someone saw a soldier entering this house. I am sure you know the punishment for that!"

"Please, there is no one here except my son's widow and his young daughter," Grandfather begged.

"I don't believe you!" the voice roared back at Grandfather. "Don't try to talk your way out of this, old man!"

As the footsteps began to move around in the courtyard, another deafening round of machine guns broke out in the alley. The voices exchanged words in a panicked tone.

"We will be back," said the angry voice. "We might just finish you all off before this cold winter does. I never forget a traitor!"

"But…" Grandfather was interrupted by a loud thud. Pari instinctively got up, but her mother and Aaila pulled her back down.

"No!" the soldier said in an authoritarian voice.

Pari sat back down with a heavy heart. They heard more voices, threatening voices, the shuffling of feet and finally, after what felt like an eternity, they waited some more, and that is when they heard the screeching sound of the courtyard's gate closing. Pari's heart filled with hope. "Grandfather is okay," she whispered quietly.

An intermittent grinding sound of wood against the frozen ground approached the tiny dark room. Pari could recognize the sound of her grandfather's crutches from any distance. She smiled in the dark and focused her vision precisely on the opening of the room. A dark shadow appeared, and his silver beard glowed faintly in the dark. *Everything blended in with the darkness in the background, like a black canvas, as if an angry painter had smeared black paint all over the cloth but missed a small little stubborn white spot,* Pari thought.

"It is safe to come out now," Grandfather carefully whispered. "They are gone."

16

Pari lit the oil lantern. Aalia and her mother carried chunks of wood to load the stove. As they all entered the room, Pari, holding the lantern, she noticed a large bruise on Grandfather's forehead. She gasped in dismay.

"Did the cowards do that to you?" she asked, feeling angry and guilty at the same time. *I should have run out to his aid when I heard all those noises*, she thought.

"It is nothing," said Grandfather with a frown on his face "The wound I have suffered all these years is far worse than this." He gestured to the woman soldier who was still there, to sit down on the mattress closest to the woodstove. Pari's mother spread a square piece of plastic on the floor and in the middle of it, placed a few pieces of *naan* (flatbread), small glasses, and a tiny bowl filled with sugar. Most of the nights, dinner consisted of sweet hot tea and bread. Looking at the bread, all of a sudden, Pari jumped up and ran outside.

She just remembered that she had not seen or heard Saffron since they all hid in that tandoor room. She lit a candle outside and looked around, it was dark and she was still missing a shoe.

"Saffron, come here!" Pari yelled. "Where are you?" *What if he ran out when those murderous men came in?* Pari wondered, filled with anger. "Remember, I promised to keep you safe," Pari pleaded as she tried hard not to cry. "I am sorry for leaving you behind."

A little shuffling noise came from the direction of the barberry bush. Pari froze. She resented that plant, it always brought back those horrible memories. She hesitantly approached it. The candle flame swayed side by side every time the wind blew, casting moving shadows on the mud walls. She tried to just look ahead and ignore the shadows. As she got closer to the barberry bush, she noticed two tiny glowing eyes looking at her from underneath the intertwined leafless branches.

"Saffron! Come here!" Pari crouched down as Saffron jumped into her arms. With all the excitement, Pari dropped the candle and hugged Saffron tight and showered him with kisses.

"You were hiding from them too?" Pari asked, entering the room. When she stepped into the room, she noticed the soldier had taken her helmet off. Her red, curly hair reached to her shoulders, and in contrast to her red hair, her eyes seemed even greener than before. *She looks beautiful*, Pari thought. She carefully put Saffron down, but he did not move and stayed close to her.

"Pari, how did you find him?" Pari's mother shook her head in despair. "Didn't I tell you that we can't feed him? Are you going to feed him bread every day?" And now, for the first time, she noticed that Pari was missing a shoe.

"Oh *Khuda Jan* (dear God), what happened to your shoe?" she asked, looking worried. "Let me see, your foot is bleeding," she continued.

"I will tell you all about it later." Pari's voice trembled. She did not want to remember again all that happened by recounting it to them. She wanted to tuck away those horrifying moments somewhere in the far part of her memory.

"Come sit next to me," Aalia said lovingly. She always recognized that look of pain on Pari's face. The soldier looked at Pari and pointed to her foot.

"Lost shoe?" she asked.

Pari's mother dropped the glass she had just picked up to fill with tea.

"*Weee* (Yikes) she speaks Dari?" she mumbled in disbelief. Aalia and Grandfather looked surprised and their mouths hung open.

"Yes, she does a little!" Pari burst out laughing. Aalia covered her mouth and began to giggle uncontrollably and between giggles, she kept on saying, "It sounds funny!" The soldier began to laugh, too.

"My name is Kate…I have a translator friend, taught me," she continued with a smile on her face. "I know a little."

"She is a foreigner and her name is Kate!" Pari's mother looked at Grandfather and said it as loud as she could.

"I am not deaf, I heard her," Grandfather said assertively. Pari's mother still looked in shock as she adjusted her headscarf with her gaze transfixed on the soldier.

Pari looked at the soldier and pointed to herself, "Pari." Then she pointed at everyone as she went around the room. "Aalia, mother," and as she pointed to Grandfather, he smiled and introduced himself, "Samad," saying it he put his hand on his heart as a sign of respect and sincerity.

Kate looked at everyone and nodded her head. Pari looked at her with awe. She was a woman, not much taller than Pari herself, with relatively small stature, but she was a brave and strong soldier. As the oil lamp cast its dancing light on her face, her eyes sparkled and accentuated the curls of her hair. Pari looked at her admiringly.

"I have curly hair, too," she said quietly under her breath. For the first time, she loved her curly hair. The soldier just smiled, probably not understanding what Pari had said.

"I used to go to school, but I can't any longer," Pari said loudly, "they burned my school." Everyone looked at her with surprise. Even Pari did not know why she blurted it out. She felt embarrassed. The room was warmer than usual and it felt good. Pari noticed her mother was putting more wood in the stove than the usual ration for the night. *She wants to keep our guest warm*, Pari thought. Saffron laid lazily on his back by Pari and every time Pari moved slightly, he looked up immediately to make sure she was not going anywhere. Aalia and mother fell into deep thought. Aalia appeared much older than her actual age. Grandfather rested his head against the wall and tried to ignore the throbbing pain in his forehead. He looked at the soldier and smiled at her, and the soldier smiled back at him.

Grandfather looked at Pari with love and gestured her to come to sit next to him. Pari got up, and with limping Saffron in tow, nestled down by her grandfather's side.

"This is when language, nationality, borders, religion all melt away and humanity and love take over," said Grandfather looking at Pari. "Sometime you don't have to speak the same language in order to understand each other. Humanity has no specific language," he said, staring into space. A sense of fear, anxiety, and panic lingered in the room. *What if those men come back?* Pari wondered, filled with fear. She looked at the soldier's hands, tightly wrapped around her weapon. *She is probably afraid too, being alone with strangers in a strange country,* Pari thought.

The crackling sound of the soldier's radio startled everyone. Pari's mother said a prayer loudly. The soldier muttered some words as she held the radio close to her mouth. She sprang to her feet and looked at everyone with gratitude. She walked up to Grandfather and shook his hand firmly. She walked to Aalia and Pari's mother to shake their hands, but as they extended their hands, the soldier threw her arms up in the air and hugged them instead.

"Thank you..." she said, trying to sound tough, but Pari could see the tears glistening in her eyes. She patted Pari on the head and hugged her tightly.

"You brave...don't change," she said as she winked at Pari.

"Stay here...no come outside!" she ordered as she swiftly exited the mudroom.

17

Aalia wanted to get back home to her little daughter, Afsana. She had already stayed longer than she should have. Enough time had elapsed since the soldier left, but no one wanted to go outside and check. The sense of fear and panic always escalated at night.

"I will go and check." Pari got up and walked outside with bare feet.

As Pari stepped outside, the cold air took her breath away. There was nothing but darkness outside. The wind was blowing hard, and from time to time, it picked up some of the snow off the ground and dragged it along. It was like the monster of darkness was in an unwanted dance with the snow fairy, hauling it around, unwillingly. Pari hated the darkness, every night the darkness breathed life into her fears and nightmares, and tonight the kind soldier had evaporated into darkness. Pari knew her fellow soldiers were waiting for the right moment to rescue her, but that thought did not comfort her at all. She sighed out loud.

As she turned around to step back inside, she stumbled upon something. She bent down, searching with her hands to find the objects she had almost tripped over. As soon as she lifted them up, she realized that they were the soldier's boots. Her eyes were filled with tears.

"Pari, where are you?" Aalia walked out, holding a candle.

"Look, she left her boots for me, Aalia," Pari's voice shook with emotion as she held up the soldier's boots for Aalia to see.

Later that night, Pari told her mother and grandfather about everything that happened that day. She told them about the kind blacksmith, the explosion, finding Saffron and how the friendly soldier had come to her help.

Upon learning of Pari's head wound, her mother had a hard time taking the scarf off Pari's head. Each time she pulled it, Pari screamed in pain.

Dried up blood from a big laceration made the headscarf stick to her head.

That night, even though everyone lay on their thin mattresses on the floor pretending to sleep, no one could go to sleep. Grandfather coughed and moaned in pain more often than before. The voices of those men echoed in his ears over and over again. Their merciless faces kept on taunting him and laughing at him, pointing fingers and calling him "the landmine sniffing dog!" It filled him with resentment and rage.

Pari struggled hard to free her mind from the daunting memories of that day. Each time she closed her eyes, they came back like roaring murky floodwater, sweeping her back into a dark, deep abyss. The sound of the explosion kept on ringing in her ears; the images came back to life, dancing in front of her eyes. The spice storeowner's dust and spice covered face, mumbling incoherently, kept on swinging back and forth in the darkness of the room. Pari pulled her patched-up quilt over her eyes and forcefully shut her eyes. Once she finally fell asleep, she dreamed she was sitting with her father in a beautiful meadow, covered with fragrant white lilies. The sun was shining bright and her father was reading a story from her favorite book, and to her surprise, the book's last pages were no longer missing. Pari was filled with excitement and anticipation. Finally, she was about to find out how the story ended. But all of a sudden, the sky grew dark and angry. Pari looked around. The sun was whisked away by a strong gust of wind. The white lilies had turned into a thick layer of snow, "Father!" she screamed in fear and turned to him. But he was no longer sitting next to her. The book sat on the ground. She picked it up and frantically leafed through the pages until she got to the last few ones. She gasped with disappointment. The pages were blank. All of a sudden, a powerful gust of wind blew the book out of her hands. Pari tried to reach it, but the wind carried it farther and farther from her. She began to run after it, but she was not fast enough. The snow was slippery and cold as she attempted to run faster. She watched the book get smaller and smaller in the far distance until she tripped and fell into a ditch. She was too tired and cold to crawl back out. She curled up there and sobbed.

"Are you okay?" came a voice from the edge of the ditch. Pari looked up, and there was her father sitting there looking down at her.

"The wind stole my book," Pari cried with relief now that her father was there to help her. "I did not get to read the ending." Pari cried harder. Her father looked down at her with a loving smile.

"You always came up with a different ending each time we read it together. Sometimes it is better if you get to choose how the story ends," he said as he reached out to her.

Pari grabbed his hand tightly and climbed out of the ditch. Once out, she looked up, expecting to see her father. But instead, there stood the kind soldier. "You are brave," she said.

"Father!" Pari screamed and began to sob once again.

"Don't cry, my child. Wake up!" her mother said. Pari woke up. Her mother's voice was like a spear that shattered that suffocating glass castle of nightmares that had imprisoned her for what felt like an eternity.

18

The next few days, Pari stayed inside. She did not leave the little room. She refused to go out to the courtyard. The sight of snow made her sick to her stomach. The squeaking sounds of the door filled her with anxiety and fear. She covered her ears and grinded her teeth with each loud noise. Her mother and grandfather exchanged worried looks, and sometimes, grandfather went to the tandoor room and talked to her mother while she baked bread.

Saffron did not leave her side either. She tried to wash the spice out of his fur, but that stubborn yellow hue still clung to his fur.

"Well, you have to stay true to your name," Pari said, stroking his back. "I hope you stay yellow forever."

Grandfather gave Saffron a lot of love. At times, he even shared his bread with him. Saffron knew how to give him a sad puppy look in order to get more food.

Grandfather was more accepting of keeping him once he found out Saffron had a limp.

"He is just like me!" he said with a smile, stroking his back. Sometimes Pari watched Saffron playing in the snow from the small window of the room.

He loved climbing on the tall mounds of the snow that had clung to the walls of the courtyard. Sometimes he blended in with the snow so well that had it not been for his yellowish fur, it would have been hard to spot him. Saffron often stood in front of the barberry bush and stared at it for minutes. Watching him from the window, it made Pari feel anxious. The tall snow covered the barberry bush. It appeared to her as a leaning, angry monster, waiting to entrap the unsuspecting little dog standing in front of it.

"No, Saffron! Don't get any closer!" she whispered, pressing her forehead against the wooden frame of the small window.

"Come back here!" Pari yelled, tapping on the windowpane. At times, Pari would run to the door and urge Saffron with a scolding tone to move away from the barberry bush. Each time he would obediently run back to her with his little ears flopping back and forth. Saffron rarely barked and that was puzzling to Pari. Maybe he was always frightened and hid away from people. It was safer to be invisible, Pari thought.

Days passed before Aalia climbed down the ladder into Pari's courtyard. She looked pale and distressed.

She just sat on the mattress and did not speak much. Pari's heart filled with sadness and anguish. Maybe like me, Aalia fears the return of those men. *Maybe if I had not gone out that day none of this would have happened*, Pari thought.

Grandfather sat by the woodstove. Pari's mother's labored over her old sewing machine. The sewing machine resembled an old animal made out of steel, Pari thought relentlessly, biting pieces of cloth, it left little teeth marks as it ran underneath it.

"Aalia tell me a story, please," Pari asked. Aalia, still deep in thought, did not respond. Pari's grandfather looked at both of them with concern.

"Aalia, my child, is everything okay?" He asked, sounding worried.

Aalia looked up and shook her head.

"Well, since our storyteller seems a little tired, maybe I can tell you two a story today," Grandfather chuckled. Both Aalia and Pari looked up at him with surprise. Pari's mother's sewing machine came to a halt. She walked up to them and sat next to Pari. After making herself comfortable, she smiled at grandfather and gestured to him to begin. Grandfather coughed a few times, and after clearing his throat, he began:

Once upon a time in a faraway land, under the turquoise blue sky and on the emerald green pastures, existed a kingdom of a very kind Sultan. The kingdom was happy and prosperous. Clear sweet water flowed in rivers. The tall golden wheat fields shone from afar, and the trees stood tall and proud, bearing ripe fruits. The Sultan was kind, fair, and loved by all the inhabitants of his land. He was blessed with a daughter whom he loved dearly and treasured more than his entire kingdom. The Sultan often walked the hallways of the palace with the princess by his side, sharing stories and laughter. Sometimes they just sat on the balcony enjoying the beauty and vastness of his Kingdom.

One day when the princess had just turned sixteen, the Sultan went hunting to a forest fairly close to the palace. The Sultan and his men, riding on horses, entered the dense forest, disturbing the tranquility and peacefulness. The rabbits, fawns, and all the other animals began to run away. The Sultan and his men rode deep into the forest. They came upon a deer and a fawn feeding on the dewy green leaves of a tree. The Sultan and his men got off their horses and gingerly tiptoed toward the deer and her fawn. The arrows were placed in the bows as everyone awaited the Sultan to release the first arrow. As the Sultan stretched the bowstring, a shuffling noise coming from the top of the tree startled him, and he erroneously released the arrow. The deer and the fawn looked up, hesitated for a few seconds, and then hurriedly ran, disappearing into the forest. The sound of an object falling from the tree and hitting the ground prompted the Sultan to go closer to take a look. Maybe it was a squirrel, he thought. The sounds of the leaves being crushed under his boots seemed ominous. Once he reached the bottom of that majestic old tree, he felt dwarfed in comparison to the tree trunk, the biggest he had ever laid eyes on. He saw a toppled nest with few broken eggs lying on the ground, some with visible little feathers piercing through the cracks of the eggshells. The Sultan knelt down, feeling remorse and sadness. As he tried to pick up a broken egg, a black bird with gigantic wings flew down and pecked at the back of his hand. The frightened Sultan stepped back and stared at the bird with astonishment. The bird's eyes were red and glowed like fire. Her wings were amazingly vast. The arrow from Sultan's bow had pierced one wing. When she flapped her wings, the arrow swayed from side to side. The Sultan's men were frozen in fear, still holding their bows and arrows. The giant bird looked at the cracked eggs and her damaged nest and took a step toward the Sultan. As the Sultan tried to take a step back, he stumbled and fell. He tried not to look at the black bird. Its enormity and red eyes sent a chill down his spine. The bird took another step closer to him, and then in a voice that shook the forest, she roared.

"You will pay for this!" she hissed. "I put a curse on your offspring. May she never be able to set foot outdoors! If she ever does, she will be attacked and shredded into pieces! Beware of my revenge!" she bellowed as she stared right into the Sultan's eyes. Then as suddenly as she had appeared, she flapped her wings and vanished instantly. The leaves and branches shook violently and the swarm of birds took flight out of the forest, darkening the sky like black storm clouds.

The Sultan and his men dazed and scared, got back on their horses, and hurried toward the palace. The Sultan's heart was pounding with fear. Even though he had seen the black bird fly away, he felt a dark presence following him and hovering overhead.

As soon as the Sultan got back to the palace, he ordered his guards and soldiers to lock down all doors and windows. He rushed to the queen's chamber to share the horrific news with her and the princess. Both the Sultan and queen decided it would be best to prevent the princess from going outdoors. The Sultan stopped taking walks outside in the garden with his beloved daughter, and he no longer sat on the balcony surrounded by intricate railings, to admire the beauty of his kingdom. He walked alone in the hallways of the palace and often mumbled to himself. A swarm of black birds perched daily on the rooftops of the palace, like a black sinister entity suffocating the inhabitants of the palace. The princess stayed in her room often, and as time went by, she refused to come out at all. Watching his daughter suffer and wither away took a toll on the Sultan's health. He often spoke to himself and sometimes he crouched in an attempt to avoid an invisible bird flying overhead.

A sense of sadness and despair took over the kingdom. A veil of hopelessness covered the princess's face. She sat by her window, like a statue frozen in time. Seasons changed, and the window to her room was like a picture frame through which the passage of time and seasons was recorded.

One day on a warm spring day, as the princess sat by the window, a beautiful butterfly landed on the windowsill. Its antennae wiggled and the wings vibrated in the wind. The strong gusts of the wind failed to move the little butterfly. It sat there unaffected and strong-willed. The princess watched the little butterfly intently, studying it closely. Hours passed, the delightful butterfly fought every gust and hung in there with the wind mercilessly moving its wings back and forth.

"It is better to die free and fight for freedom," the princess whispered. She sprang to her feet, rushing toward her bedroom door. She flew down numerous steps. At times, stumbling and losing balance. As she got to the main gate, she ordered the guards to open it. The guards refused to obey, but in a blink of an eye, the princess snatched the sword of one of the guards and ordered him to open the gates. They hesitantly opened the gate, as some of them dispersed to sound the alarm. The princess stepped outside for the first time in two years. She loved it as the warm rays of the sun stroked her face. She breathed the air in with much joy. She stood there looking up at the sky, twirling around with excitement. Suddenly a swarm of black birds appeared overhead. It seemed like a dark patch of clouds heading towards her, getting ready to whisk her away. The screams and gasps of the people got increasingly louder, among which she could recognize her father's desperate cry.

"Come back in, my love!" he begged her. "You can't be out there! The black birds will snatch you away! Please listen to me!" he pleaded.

The princess just stood there as hundreds of black birds landed on the ground. A few were circling around overhead. The princess was not afraid. She did not want to live the rest of her life in fear and isolation.

"I am not afraid of you!" she screamed at the top of her lungs. "You want to shred me into pieces? Go ahead. Peck at me and snatch me away!" she stared the birds in the eyes and stubbornly stood there. The queen was sobbing as the Sultan tried to order the soldiers to aim at the birds, but there were thousands of them.

"No!" the princess shouted. "No one is to touch their bows and arrows," she said firmly! "It is my order and you need to obey it."

The birds stayed, staring at her, the others continued to circle overhead. The princess stared back.

"I refuse to be afraid!" she whispered to herself over and over again.

All of a sudden, the birds circling overhead dispersed into different directions, and the ones on the ground took flight as if a big gust of wind blew them away. The birds sitting on the rooftop of the palace flew away and for the first time in two years, one could finally see the green color of the palace's rooftop.

Everyone began to rejoice and a sense of euphoria and bliss replaced the fear and sadness that had enslaved everyone for years. People believed the princess's bravery broke the curse. She faced her fears and that was the catalyst to reclaiming her freedom. Once again, happiness prevailed in the kingdom. The Sultan was seen taking long walks with his daughter in the palace gardens with the princess wearing a bejeweled butterfly necklace that she never parted with.

Pari was so engrossed in the story that she never noticed the sun was already hiding behind the mountains. Its last rays stubbornly attempted to fight the darkness of the dusk, but the fast-approaching night dragged a curtain of blackness as it crept through the village, covering it slowly.

The little oil lantern was already lit, the shadow of the flame dancing on the mud walls of the small room. Aalia was as deep in thought as she had appeared when she first came. The smoke stained kettle was humming on the woodstove, the steam coming out of its spout, like a baby dragon.

"How did you like the story Pari?" Grandfather asked between coughs.

"I loved it, the princess was so brave. How did you like it, Aalia?" Pari said as she looked at Aalia, who suddenly sprang to her feet.

"Once again, I lost track of time. I should have been home a long time ago." Aalia quickly ran to the door and hurriedly put her shoes on. She said goodbye and disappeared into the darkness outside.

That was strange. I wonder why Aalia acts so peculiarly sometimes. Pari thought.

That night as Aalia lay next to her little daughter, her mind was restless with worries and thoughts. She stroked Afsana's hair as she slept peacefully.

"I will never let anyone take you away from me, my love," she whispered to Afsana softly. "I don't want these four mud walls to be your only companions as you grow up." She lifted up Afsana's little hand and kissed her tiny black fingers over and over again. Lately, Afsana had gotten into the habit of taking small pieces of coal out of the stove and using it to draw on the walls. "You are my princess, and I will not let my fears or anyone else's make you a prisoner," Aalia said softly. "I will not let your father, the big black birds, the crows or vultures take you away from me."

As Afsana continued to sleep peacefully, Aalia kept on mumbling to herself, "not the big black birds, not the crows or the vultures…not the big black birds, not the crows, not the vultures…" and she repeated it again and again until finally sleep weighed her eyelids down and helped her drift away.

Only a short distance away in another little mud house, Pari lay on her back as she thought about the big black birds with glowing red eyes and the brave princess. She imagined herself standing in the courtyard looking at the surrounding walls on which sat big black birds but their heads belonged to the turban-wearing men. They all had red eyes and held guns in their beaks. Pari fearlessly released an arrow at each one's direction as they all toppled down to the ground, one by one. Pari smiled and turned to her side and pulled the old quilt up to her chin. It was getting bitterly cold in the room. The little heap of wood was shrinking in size as the cold of winter consumed it eagerly one by one. She lifted up her head and looked at Saffron, who slept soundlessly. It seemed like a white lump of glowing white snow in the darkness of the room.

Pari woke up to the shuffling sounds of someone's shoes outside. Her heart skipped a beat as she froze in fear. She listened intently, hoping she was wrong, her heartbeat echoed in her ears as she tried to focus on the sounds. She lifted her body halfway on her elbows and looked around the room. Saffron was standing by the door with his ears perked up. Seeing that, Pari felt even more terrified.

"Come here, Saffron," she tried to whisper, but the pitch of her voice went up and down with nervousness, "Please don't bark."

Saffron looked at Pari and slowly limped toward her. Pari got up. Picking him up swiftly, she cautiously tiptoed to the window. It was still dark outside, but the glow of snow-covered ground made the courtyard light up like a full moon night.

Pari looked outside, praying no one was there and that she had just imagined the sound. Everything seemed eerie. She pressed her forehead against the cold glass of the little window in an attempt to see more clearly. That was when she saw a shadow-like figure approaching the house and a sharp squeal escaped her throat. She hastily moved away from the window and put Saffron down. Worried she may have awakened her mother and grandfather, she glanced at them. They both were still asleep. *It's all in my imagination*, she thought. There is nothing out there. She decided to take one more look outside. She slowly moved toward the window and looked outside. The courtyard was empty. The sound of the wind sneaking through the cracks of the wooden window frame resembled a soft continuous whistle.

"See it is nothing, Saffron, just the wind," she whispered, looking down at Saffron, who was standing very close to her feet, ears still perked up. As Pari was about to move away from the window, she caught a glimpse of someone standing right there, looking at her behind the glass pane. She was shocked and thought she was seeing her long-dead father.

"Father," she exclaimed in disbelief. There stood her father on the snow, his pale face covered in a love-filled smile. She felt mesmerized and frozen with fear at the same time. *This is not possible*, she thought. Her head swam around with disbelief. She quickly wiped up the foggy glass with her sleeve, hoping her eyes were playing a trick on her. But with each swipe, the figure standing there became clearer. She wasn't imagining it after all. She wanted to run outside and hug him tight and never let go of him, but then she was afraid to let him out of her sight and lose him, lose him again. She wanted to run to her mother and grandfather and wake them up but was afraid to move away from the window. She couldn't divert her sight away from him. She was transfixed.

Her father took few steps forward, and put his hand on the window, Pari put hers on his hand from the other side of the glass. She wept soundlessly.

"I miss you, Father," she sobbed. "I miss you a lot. Please stay here with me forever. We are so hopeless without you."

Her father looked at her with tenderness. "You are the bravest girl I have ever known, Pari," her father said, smiling at her. "Do you remember the 'chase the light' game we used to play when you were very young?"

Pari looked at him with surprise, as she wiped her tears. "Of course I remember," she responded, almost in a whisper. All of a sudden, Pari found herself standing in the corner of the little room as if transported back in time. It felt like that passage of time had reversed, and taken her on a stroll down memory lane. She was about four years old, watching herself curled up in her father's arms and crying. Nothing her father or mother did could console her. She was deeply shaken by the sound of an explosion nearby, and she had clung to her father, refusing to let go. Her father got up, with Pari still hanging on to him, lowered the light of the kerosene lamp until the flame died out completely, and darkness invaded the room. He then took out a small flashlight and began to shine it on the mud wall of the small room. "Look, Pari," he said as he gently kissed the top of her head. "You, see the light? Now, show me if you can catch it. I don't think mother and grandfather are fast enough to do it. But I have a feeling your little feet are fast enough to do so." He grinned as he put Pari down on the floor. Pari hesitantly let go of him and wiped her hair away from her face. She shyly looked at her mother and grandfather, who began to cheer her on. "Go fly, my little fairy," Grandfather hollered.

"You can do it." Pari smiled and eagerly sprinted toward the little floating circle that glowed on the wall. Her father moved the flashlight up and down, but each time Pari was able to tag the light. Everyone laughed and clapped for her. She stood there like a shadow, cherishing the moments' gift to her by some elusive force she failed to comprehend.

"Pari," her father's voice transported her back to the small window, her hand still resting on the glass on top of his.

"Every darkness is defeated by light. You continue to chase the light, my child. It is time to chase it outside these four walls. Chase it on the dark canvas of your fears. Don't let fear stop you. Chase your light until you catch it, and catch it forever."

Pari nodded in agreement with tears still running down her cheeks.

He looked at her with affection and began to slowly walk away.

"No, please don't go, please..." Pari cried inconsolably. Once back in the middle of the courtyard, he came to a halt, turned around and looked back at Pari.

"Please, please stay," Pari pleaded in a whisper. He kept on walking and, once by the barberry bush, he vanished.

Pari's knees gave in and she slumped onto the floor. She felt dizzy and was in utter disbelief. She struggled to make sense of everything that had just happened. Was this all a dream, she wondered. Saffron sat by her patiently as she sat on the floor, holding her head between her hands. Every now and then he licked her hand.

19

That night, as Pari finally lay back on her mattress, she was jolted by a thunderous sound of someone pushing the door open. She screamed in fear. "Mother! Grandfather! "That is when she saw the figure of a turban-wearing man holding a gun standing in the doorway. The man barged in the room, pointing his gun at Grandfather, who still lay on his mattress.

"Who are you?" Grandfather's voice shook with fear as he struggled to sit up on his mattress. "Why are you here?" he seemed disoriented as he tried to shield his eyes with his hand from the harsh light of the flashlight. "Please do not hurt us," he begged.

Pari's mother pulled Pari toward her and held her tight. She began to pray quietly. Pari felt her mother's body tremble.

"Get up, you cripple!" The man bellowed with rage. "You are a traitor. I knew very well. That day you were full of crap!" He continued with disgust. You sheltered that soldier and then had the guts to lie about it!"

"In the name of God, please do not hurt us." Pari's mother shrieked with fright. "We are innocent, poor people," she pleaded as she began to sob. "We are your own people. We have not done anything wrong."

The gunman pointed the flashlight at Pari and her mother, both sitting on the floor huddled together. Pari sank her face in her mother's arms to avoid the glaring light. She tried not to cry, but she could feel the tears welling up in her eyes. *It's all my fault,* she thought. *We all will be killed.*

"Shut your mouth, woman! Or I will put a bullet in it! You filthy, worthless liar." The man's rage-filled rant sent chills down Pari's spine. Her mother put her hand over her mouth to muffle the sound as she cried.

"Are you a spy?" The man asked with fury. "Do you work for foreigners? What happened to the soldier?"

"No, we are not spies, son," but before Grandfather could finish his sentence, the gunman hit him on the forehead with the butt of his gun. Grandfather moaned in pain.

"I am not here to listen to your lies, old man. You fess up now, or you and your family will be first flogged publicly then stoned to death! That is how we deal with traitors."

Pari's mother let out a cry of despair. Pari could see the blood trickling down Grandfather's forehead and it filled her with rage. She clenched her fists and grinded her teeth with anger. She looked around the room quickly. Dawn was approaching and a dim light was slowly entering the room through the small window. She noticed something metallic reflecting the light from the flashlight. She squinted hard. It was the metal part on her grandfather's crutch. She gingerly scooted closer and stretched her arm as far as she could.

The gunman ordered the grandfather. "Get up!" he taunted with disdain. "Unless you want to lose the other leg too!" The gunman shone the light around the room and suddenly stopped as he had noticed something of significance. Pari followed his gaze and her heart sank with terror as soon as she realized what the gunman was staring at. The boots, now engulfed by the light, sat by the wall. The gunman furiously walked up to Grandfather and pulled him up by his collar.

"Please! I can explain. My family had nothing to do with this!" He begged over and over again as the gunman kept on slamming his frail body against the wall. Pari covered her ears and closed her eyes in anguish and she screamed as loudly as she could. "Leave him alone! I did it! I brought the soldier home!"

The gunman startled by her outburst, stopped and gave her a resentful look. He slammed grandfather against the wall one more time before throwing him to the ground. Pari's mother threw herself in front of Pari, who sat there staring back at the man.

"She is lying," she pleaded. "She had nothing to do with it! It's my fault. I did it all. Please take me!" she tried to stop the gunman who was now staring at Pari.

"So you did it?" he snarled "You worthless, filthy girl!"

"Yes, I did it!" Pari said with contempt. "She saved my life! I am not afraid and I do not regret doing it!"

"Is she going to come to your rescue again?" the gunman said in a mocking voice. "Where is your soldier friend now? Why don't you call her to save you?" he taunted her as he stepped closer and closer.

Pari's body was beginning to get limp with fear, her knees were shaking and her hands were sweating. She tried to breathe normally. I am not afraid. She tried to convince herself. But her heart and mind were not working in synch as her breathing was becoming more and more rapid, and her heart throbbed frantically.

"My father told me that I was braver than anyone he knew, "Pari shouted at the gunman "I will save my own life this time!" Saying that, Pari swiftly lifted up grandfather's crutch and struck the gunman in the face. The unexpected blow to his face made the gunman stumble backward and before he could balance himself, another blow to the head caused him to collapse on the floor. That is when Saffron leaped from behind the wood stove and latched onto the gunman's hand.

20

Aalia combed Afsana's hair, her hidden little girl. She braided it neatly while little Afsana played with the old comb that was missing most of its teeth. She kept on sticking her little finger in the gaps that were created by broken teeth.

"Broken?" she looked at her mom inquisitively, pointing to the gaps.

"Yes," Aaila replied.

"Why?" asked little Afsana.

"Because the comb is getting old and worn out," Aalia explained.

"Just like Grandma?" Afsana interrupted.

"Yes, just like Grandma. She is getting old and losing her teeth, too." Aalia smiled at Afsana.

"I am hungry," Afsana announced as she got up to her feet once she realized she was free from the hair combing session.

"We will have some bread and tea…"Aalia offered as she walked over to the stove.

"No," little Afsana protested. "I want rice, brown rice!"

Aalia's heart ached with sadness. Now that Afsana was almost three, she expressed her wants much more often. Food was to be rationed wisely. Aalia's mother worked as a maid, and every now and then, she brought some leftovers home. It was a welcome change from the usual bread and tea.

"Maybe rice for later," Aalia promised hesitantly. "But guess what?" Aalia looked at Afsana with love. "I am going to take you to a friend's house!" she exclaimed with excitement. Afsana's eyes widened with eagerness and she began to run in circles shrieking with zeal. Seeing Afsana's exhilaration, Aalia's heart filled with joy. *I want to give you all the happiness under the blue sky*, she thought as Afsana began to tumble on the floor.

Aalia hoisted Afsana up the wooden ladder, making sure her little feet were landing on the bars of the ladder and not slipping through the gaps. She had wrapped a thick blanket around Afsana's little frame to keep her warm, which made the climb more challenging.

"I fall!" Afsana kept on saying in a scared voice.

"No, I am here, right behind you. I'll catch you if you fall. I'll always be there to catch you. "Aalia reassured her over and over again. "Do you know who lives on the other side of the wall, Afsana?" Aalia asked. "My friend and Saffron," without waiting for Afsana's response, she added with excitement. Once they both descended into the snow-covered courtyard, Aalia became anxious. I hope they forgive me for keeping Afsana hidden for such a long time, she thought. Maybe they will think of me as a coward for keeping her away from everyone. I will explain everything, she finally concluded as she picked up Afsana in her arms and stepped toward the little mud house. It was unusually quiet that morning and a peculiar sense of apprehension lurked in the air. Maybe it's just me, Aalia thought as she held Afsana close to her chest and continued taking cautious steps on the snow. All of a sudden, she noticed a set of footprints. She stopped and observed them very carefully. The trail had originated from the old metal gate of the courtyard and had stopped right by the small door of the mud house. They simply cannot belong to Pari or her mother, and grandfather left only one footprint, she thought. They were too big, probably a man's she concluded as her heart skipped a beat. She reluctantly took another couple of steps and paused.

"Pari!" she yelled out loud. She waited, but there was no response. For a moment, she contemplated running back to the ladder. What if there is something wrong, I can't just leave, she decided. She began to pray as she pushed the squeaking, old door open to the house and once again called out Pari's name. Aalia gasped with dread as she noticed Pari's grandfather sitting up against the wall with a big laceration on his forehead. Before another gasp escaped her throat, Pari dragged her inside and swiftly shut the door behind her.

"Was it them?" Aalia questioned Pari frantically. "Did they come back?"

"Hush!" Pari commanded with authority as she placed her finger on her lips.

"We cannot be loud." She pointed to the tandoor room. "Speak only in whispers."

Aalia's hair raised on the back of her neck. She pressed Afsana closer to her chest. She noticed the room was dreadfully cold and the fire was not lit in the stove. There were two old duffle bags stuffed with clothes. Pari's mother sat on the mattress, despondent and motionless in a statuesque pose. Her face was pale, her eyes puffy and long scratches that ran down all the way to her neck. She quickly took another look at Pari's face. She had a purple bruise underneath her left eye. Her hair was out and the curls framed her face like a dark halo, a sorrowful halo. Pari's grandfather's grief-stricken eyes followed Pari's every move with a desolate look on his face.

"What is in the tandoor room, Pari?" Aalia whispered, not really sure if she wanted to know. Pari looked at her mother and grandfather nervously.

They just stood there in silence for what felt like an eternity until Afsana got restless and wiggled her body out of the oversized old blanket and landed on the floor. Pari looked at her with surprise. Saffron, who was by the woodstove, lifted up his head and glanced at Afsana with curiosity, wiggling his nose.

"Dog!" Afsana giggled with excitement as she pointed to Saffron. She hopped with eagerness toward Saffron, who was already hobbling in her direction with equal zeal. Momentarily, everyone seemed to have forgotten their troubles as muffled laughter broke out in the room.

"Who are you, little one?" Pari knelt down next to Afsana who was too distracted by Saffron to answer any questions. She was petting Saffron's head and he just stood there soaking up the attention.

"This is Afsana," Aalia said timidly. "My daughter."

"Your daughter?" Pari asked, looking bewildered. "When did this happen, Aaila?" Pari asked with astonishment. Pari's mother and grandfather appeared as astounded as Pari.

"Well, did you ever wonder why I always came over and you never did? Or why I always had an excuse whenever you wanted to come over?" Aalia asked, looking at Pari apologetically. "Or those months I was home sick and never visited you?" she asked.

"But why, Aalia? You did not trust me?" Pari speculated out loud.

Aalia tried to fight the tears that were quickly beginning to sting her eyes. "I have always trusted you like a little sister, but I have never had the courage to share her with the world. My life has been torturous as a woman." Aalia touched her deep scar on her forehead gently and continued, "If Afsana's father came to know of her existence, her life would not be any different from mine. I don't want her to be just a commodity in a man's household. I don't want a man to beat her up or hurt her in any way," she said with resentment. "My Afsana is going to write her own destiny, I will make sure of that and that is why I gave her that name." She looked at everyone with pride. Pari's mother got up and embraced Aalia with affection.

"Don't stop fighting for her, Aalia. It is not that you are not brave but when you have to fight everyone every step of the way, one can't help but to feel defeated." She said it in a resigned tone.

"For people like us," Pari's grandfather spoke for the first time since Aalia had entered the room, "going with the flow is essential to our survival. Once you go against the flow, you are plucked out and destroyed. But you go against the flow if you want her to have a respectful life," he pointed to Afsana, who was still gleefully rubbing Saffron's head. "This fight is not going to be just against the flow, but against the raging and angry wave which has already claimed the futures of so many innocent girls."

"I am ready to fight for her," Aalia promised. "I don't want her to scribble on the walls and grounds with a piece of coal. I want her to write on paper with a pen. Everything I was deprived of, she will have." She reluctantly walked up to Pari and held her hand between hers.

"Would you forgive me, Pari?" she asked.

Pari looked away. Aalia's sudden departures, sometimes gloominess and that long absence, made sense now. But throughout those times, she always managed to keep Pari distracted from her own problems, Pari admitted to herself.

"Of course. You will always be my friend. Do you remember the "kite and string game" we made up about our friendship?" Pari asked with a smirk on her face.

"Yes!" Aalia giggled, covering her mouth. "You were to pretend you were the kite and I was the string. You flew up high outside the walls of the courtyard to see what you wished to see. You told me about a beautiful, peaceful city on the top of a mountain, where everyone was happy. Pages of books hung from each tree branch instead of leaves...."

"And each time I picked a page with a story on it and brought it back to you," Pari interrupted, "and if the story was not to your liking, you were the kite and I was the string!" Pari hugged Aalia tightly and held her close for a few moments. She went to Afsana and picked her up.

"Do you know who I am? *Khala* (Aunty) Pari." She showered her face and head with kisses and Afsana hugged her head with excitement. This was the first time she had left the house. Seeing new faces and a furry four-legged being was all too much to handle and she shrieked with excitement.

"No, hush Afsana!" Aalia scolded her. She was worried since she still did not know who was in the tandoor room.

21

A sudden and loud grunt coming from the outside startled everyone. A sense of doom pierced the air and a woven net of fears trapped their spirits. Everyone became silent and looked at each other with distress.

"We need to hurry and leave!" Pari's mother began to stuff some bread into the duffle bag. "The rest of them will come back for us to finish us off!" She mumbled while her hands trembled.

"Who is in there, Pari?" Aalia asked. "What happened last night?" She felt guilty for not listening to Pari as soon as she came. Instead, she told them about her secret.

"The beast is tied up in there." Pari declared with pride. She then proceeded to recount the events of the previous night. She told Aalia how she had fought the gunman with Grandfather's crutch and the blow was so hard that it had knocked the man unconscious.

"And then they both tied his arms and legs and dragged him to the tandoor room," Grandfather pointed to Pari and her mother, who was busy taking clothes and her burqa off a big nail dug into the wall. "And I pulled a burlap sack over his rotten head!" Grandfather said with abhorrence.

"We thought about killing him," Pari confessed. "We have his gun. But we used it for knocking him unconscious one more time during the night when he began to scream."

"I stuffed my chador in his mouth," Pari's mother said with resentment.

Aalia stood there in shock and disbelief.

"What now?" she asked with panic in her voice. "He can free himself and come back to finish the job? Or he could go and bring the rest of them here. You should have finished him off!"

"That is why we have to run away. Escape from here." Pari announced. "What? But where to, Pari?" Aalia asked, almost in tears. Her heart sank. I can't lose my only friend, she thought as the lump in her throat grew bigger.

Aalia very well knew what "escape" implied. People in the village used that word more often than any other. It was that beast that visited almost every household in that war-torn country. It lurked there right by the door, knowing that the demons of war and poverty will eventually push people out of their homes and once out and in his mercy, the end was decided by how hard they fought that monster. Some made it out of his clutches and some simply died. Sometimes it all depended if anyone came to their rescue. Aalia shivered with fear.

"What? But where to Pari?" Aalia inquired, almost in tears.

"I don't know," Pari shrugged her shoulders. "Maybe a place with good people who will be kind to us. A place where I would be allowed to go to school."

"How about a place where we can go to sleep with a full stomach and sleep through the night without waking up to the sounds of explosions and guns." Aalia chimed in.

"A place where the stove never runs out of wood in winter and the room is always warm," Pari said, pointing to the stove as she smiled mischievously at her friend.

"A place where a girl can be anything she wants to be. A teacher, a doctor, or a soldier." Aalia said, smiling back at Pari.

"A place…" Pari began to say but was abruptly cut off by her mother's stern voice.

"We need to move fast," her mother said. "We cannot waste any time, Pari."

Everything was becoming so real so fast, Pari thought. Deep inside, she was filled with anxiety and fear. She looked around at the room with uncertainty. *This is it,* she thought. *This is where I was born. This is where my father played with me, loved me, and taught me. This is where he told me stories*, she pondered.

Pari ran to her old mattress that still lay on the floor and lifted up the edge and quickly picked up her only old storybook, the one with missing pages. She walked over to the faded duffle bag and enthusiastically placed the book in it. She moved the contents around. Sighing with relief, she realized there was enough room for Saffron.

Grandfather struggled up to his foot as he leaned on the wall for support. Aalia and Pari exchanged worried looks. Pari got her grandfather's hat, and with caution, put it on his head.

"Pull it over the cut." Her grandfather guided Pari's hands gently in hiding the wound. He put his warm coat on and wrapped his old shawl tightly around his body. Pari's mother buttoned up her old sweater with patched up holes and put on her burqa. Aalia stood there in a daze. *And their whole life fitted in just two old bags*, she thought sadly.

"I think it is dangerous to leave from the front door," she suggested as she walked over to Afsana, who was trying to feed Saffron an old piece of bread she had found on the floor. "You should come over to our house and leave from there. If you leave from your house, it might look suspicious. You never know. Every small window has curious eyes peering through them."

Pari and her mother looked at grandfather worriedly. He nodded his head in approval. "That is a good idea, you two go with Aalia, and I will exit the house through the front door. It would be difficult for me to climb the ladder with one leg." He said, pointing to his missing leg.

"I can help you," Pari said. "I can carry your crutches and Saffron without any problems!" She exclaimed with determination. "I am strong."

"What do you mean you can carry Saffron, Pari?" her mother asked with surprise. "We cannot take him with us," she said firmly.

This is not going to end well, Aalia thought. She knew how attached Pari had become to Saffron. Aalia looked at Pari with worry and sympathy. The color drained from Pari's face.

"What? That is so cruel, Mother," she protested. "They will come here and kill him or kick him back out into the alley!" she yelled out loud. She scooped Saffron from the floor and gave her mother a defiant look. Saffron dug his head under Pari's armpit. He did not like loud noises and he felt something was wrong. He began to shake. Pari's outburst frightened little Afsana too. She began to cry and ran into Aalia's arms.

"Shush, everyone!" Aalia looked at Pari and pointed toward the tandoor room. She held Afsana in her arms and tried to console her.

Pari stood there with defiance as tears streamed down her face. She looked at her grandfather, who was watching all this unfold seemingly calmly.

"Grandfather, please, please allow me to take him with us," she begged. "I promise he will not give anyone any trouble! I will see to it!"

Grandfather stood there looking down. *Obviously, Pari has no idea how tough this journey is going to be*, he thought. *I might not make it myself, but I will see them through for as long as my old body would allow me to*. "This is not going to be easy, Pari," he said. "We are embarking on a tough journey and our survival will be determined by how invisible and soundless we can be."

"Saffron knows how to be invisible and avoid people," Pari tried to reassure him. "Mother," Pari begged. "Please tell grandfather how he was so elusive at the alley when we first spotted him?"

"Don't be childish, Pari," her mother scolded her. "We will be lucky if we can save our own lives," she looked at Pari's grandfather who shook his head at her discreetly. She stopped and decided to remain silent.

"How would you even carry him?" Aalia wondered out loud.

"Well, he can walk with us and when he is tired, I can put him in the duffle bag with his head sticking out. He is small and light." Pari looked at her mother and grandfather anxiously.

"That might work," Aalia said hesitantly, taking Pari's side. Pari looked at her with gratitude and smiled. "He could warn you of any impending danger." Aalia added.

"Yes, like a guard dog!" Pari agreed, wiping her tears with Saffron's fur, who still had his head dug in her armpit with fear.

"Look at him!" Pari's mother pointed to Saffron. "He is shaking like a leaf in the wind and you think he will guard us?" She slapped her forehead with frustration.

"Then you all go ahead and leave! I will stay here with Saffron and face what comes!" saying that, Pari slumped down on the floor.

"This is not the time to be stubborn, Pari!" Her mother said impatiently. "Do you realize what type of danger we are in? Enough is enough!"

"I know very well, Mother," Pari said. "That is all I have known all my life. The danger of going to school, the danger of going outside, the danger of not covering my head. Nothing is new here." Pari retorted with resentment.

"God! Please help us all." Pari's mother looked heavenward and sighed.

Grandfather was deep in thought. He knew Pari's affection for Saffron was immense. They just did not have time to argue over this, he decided.

"You can bring him along, but he will be your responsibility. Yours only." He looked at Pari sternly.

"What?" Pari's mother shrieked in dismay.

Pari ran to her grandfather and kissed his rough cheeks. Then she planted kisses on the back of his wrinkled hands.

"Thank you!" she said with gratitude.

Pari's mother began to mumble under her breath and placed the strap of the duffle bag over her shoulder as she pushed the other bag toward Pari. They all paused for a minute and looked silently at one another. Everyone realized there was no turning back once they all exited that mud house.

"You all go ahead and go now," Grandfather pointed to Aalia. "I will meet you at the front door of your house. Leave the door unlatched." He led the way out of the house with Pari, Aalia, and Pari's mother following closely behind. As they passed the tandoor room Pari held her breath, her mother closed her eyes and Aalia could not help but to run on her toes keeping Afsana's head covered with the blanket. Pari's grandfather came to a stop right by the tandoor room and gestured to them to move fast.

22

Aalia and Afsana climbed down the ladder to the other side of the wall and into her tiny courtyard. Pari helped her mother climb up the old wooden ladder as she prayed quietly with every step she took. She froze halfway up the ladder and refused to take another step up.

"You can do it, just don't look down," Pari tried to reassure her.

"My feet are getting caught in the burqa, Pari," she pleaded. "I can't do this." She said helplessly.

"Who puts a *burqa* on before climbing up the ladder?" Pari hissed at her quietly and thought for a minute. "Take it off and throw it over the wall," she instructed her mother. "Then you can put it back on once you have climbed down on the other side." She tried to keep her voice down and mumbled sarcastically, "Maybe you can just throw it away for good."

"What?" her mother asked, still halfway through the ladder.

"Hold on to the ladder with one hand, and take your burqa off with the other hand," Pari raised her voice. Her mother began to take the burqa off slowly and eventually threw it over the wall. Once free from it, she moved up the ladder quicker, and soon after disappeared behind the wall.

Pari paused before she could begin her own climb. She had one last thing to do. Holding Saffron, she hastily tiptoed toward the barberry bush. She could not leave without making peace with it, she thought. She came to a halt in front of it. Some branches were still covered by snow, while some had little pieces of icicles hanging from them. She knelt down on the snow in front of the bush as she caressed one of the branches.

"I hated you for so long because you reminded me of that horrible day," she whispered. "I always came to you when I was upset and you sheltered me," she choked up when she said that. "But maybe, you did it that day, too." She wondered out loud. Saffron stretched his neck in an attempt to bite an icicle from one of the low-hanging branches. As she got up, her chador was caught on one of the branches, pulling it off of her head. "Yes, I know. I don't like it either." She chuckled as she set it free from the branch.

She got up and turned around to head back toward the ladder when a loud thud coming from the tandoor room scared her terribly. She saw Grandfather coming out of the room. He buried the gun deep in the snow. Pari, wondering what her grandfather had done to the insurgent, ran toward the ladder as fast as her legs could carry her.

Pari stood behind the door and pressed her ear against the cold metal as hard she could. The cold metal stung her face and ear, but she listened intently for the approaching sound of grandfather's crutches. She opened the door as soon as she heard the grinding sound of wood against the frozen snow come to a halt in front of it.

Her grandfather looked over his shoulder and hopped in as fast as he could.

"Before leaving our house, I took the ladder down and hid it behind a mound of snow," looking at Aalia with worry, Grandfather said, "I didn't want any suspicion to fall on you."

Aalia looked at everyone and burst in tears, knowing she would lose her only friend and dear neighbors. Her efforts of keeping all those emotions inside had failed, she thought with embarrassment. "Please wait a minute." She managed to say before she ran inside with Afsana, following her like a little shadow.

Pari's mother crouched on the ground and began to sob quietly. "What will become of us?" she asked.

"Don't lose hope my child," Pari's grandfather said reassuringly. "God willing, we will make it through this one, too. A river is alive for as long as it flows. It fights boulders and rocks as it moves forward. Sometimes it overturns rocks and sometimes it flows by making a path around them." He stopped and gently tapped Pari's mother with the tip of his crutch.

"Look at me," he said, forcefully pointing to his amputated leg. "I should have given up a long time ago. But you and Pari are the reasons I go on every day. You have to fight for your daughter." He said. "We can sit here and wait for them to come back and kill us. Or stay for the next bomb to fall on our house and blow us up into pieces. We don't have that many choices. We stay, we die, we move and we might just make it."

"We might," Pari's mother repeated those words as she stared aimlessly into the space, rocking back and forth. "We might," she repeated again.

Pari stood there with her heart getting heavier and heavier, listening to their conversation. Once again, she blamed herself for what was happening to them. *It is all my fault*, she thought, fighting her tears back.

"Here," Aalia ran out of her house, holding a red knapsack. "I packed some bread and raisins for your trip." She handed it to Pari.

"Thank you. You really did not have to. You have a little one to feed." Pari said gratefully and hugged Aalia as tightly as she could. There were more tears than words as they bid farewell. Aalia promised Pari that every night she would tell Afsana the story of *The Brave Princess and The Black Birds, and The Ghost in The Wall.* "And one day she will read me stories from a book." Aalia winked at her, hoping that it would come true.

Pari showered Afsana with kisses. Afsana masterfully wiggled out of her arms to hug Saffron's head one last time.

Grandfather said a prayer, Pari's mother lowered her burqa and Pari held on to Saffron tightly as she hid her under her chador. And as they all stepped out into the alley, Aalia threw water behind them in the hopes of a smooth and safe journey. (A common ritual so the journey is as smooth as water.)

23

Pari and her mother waited outside a small brick house as grandfather spoke to an old bearded man wearing a white turban. Every now and then the man looked at Pari and her mother from the corner of his eyes. It was almost midday and Pari welcomed the warm rays of the sun shining on her cold face. They had walked for almost two hours until they reached the man's house. Grandfather said he was a friend and would be willing to help. Pari noticed grandfather handing him a piece of folded paper, the man took a look at it and then they both shook hands. Pari's shoulder was sore from carrying the duffle bag. As she took the strap off her shoulder and gently put the bag on the ground, she thought maybe that was the deed to the house and asked herself whether their house was gone forever.

Saffron was curled up comfortably inside the bag on top of a few pieces of clothing. After a few minutes lapsed, Saffron's head popped up from the top of the unzipped bag.

"Pari, hide him!" her mother warned. "No one will help us if they come to know about him."

"Don't worry. No one will get to know. I promise. Even if someone spots him, I will say it's a rabbit." Pari smirked. "He barely barks, so who would even know?"

"Really, Pari? Do you think people are that stupid to accept that he is a rabbit?" her mother scolded her angrily.

"I don't care what people say. I would do everything possible to keep him safe." Pari declared stubbornly. "Just the way you and grandfather are struggling to keep me safe." Pari's voice trembled. She put her head on her mother's shoulder as they both sat on a dry spec of land.

Her mother lifted up her burqa and looked at Pari with love. "I would do anything to keep you safe, Pari." She quickly lowered her burqa. She did not want Pari to see the fear in her face or the tears in her eyes.

Grandfather finally returned as a corner of his shawl dragged on the ground behind him covered in slush and mud. Pari realized his friend had taken everything of value that her grandfather had to help them leave the area.

"We will leave in a couple of hours," her grandfather said, "I have arranged for a truck to pick us up." He sat down beside Pari and her mother on the ground, putting his crutches neatly next to him. "We can go inside and wait. My friend was kind enough to invite us in, but I declined. I was afraid he might refuse to help us once he found out about Saffron," he said, smiling at Pari.

"Thank you," Pari said. "I am not that cold anyways. I am fine sitting here in the sun. I would rather freeze here than to give up Saffron."

They all huddled together against the wall. The house was in a quiet and remote part of the village, not too many people passed by. They fell into deep thoughts. Pari enjoyed the stillness. It meant peace. She was tired of ghastly and deafening sounds of explosions. Her mother was worried about what was to come. *Is this the tranquil lull before the storm comes and uproots all?* Grandfather pondered about the deed of their little mud house that had been just handed over to his friend, in exchange for some money and a ride.

The wind slowly picked up and its gusts took Pari's breath away. She wrapped her chador tightly around her face.

The sounds of little footsteps made all of them look to the right. A little boy, shuddering in his thin shirt and trousers carrying a smoke-stained kettle and few metal bowls, was approaching them. He stood in front of them and handed everyone a bowl.

"Father sent you some hot soup," He said, wiping his nose with the back of his sleeve.

"Thank you, son. Tell your father we are grateful." Grandfather patted his back with affection.

He ran off as soon as he filled up the last bowl. Pari dipped the hard bread in the soup and fed Saffron, who ate with much eagerness. Another hour passed before a big truck came to a stop in front of them. Pari had seen those trucks in the bazaar unloading goods and fresh produce. The top was covered with a thick brown tarp, and long wooden slats covered both sides. There were intricate and colorful paintings on the wooden parts, mostly flowers. A little boy who was probably about ten or eleven years old unlatched the tailgate and leaped to the ground, startling Pari's mother, who let out a scream. The little boy laughed heartily. Grandfather went up to the driver and spoke while Pari and her mother stood there, ready to get on the truck.

"*Salaam* (greetings), my name is Omeed (hope) and I am the driver's assistant," he announced proudly and added, "Or you can call me conductor, too."

Grandfather gestured to them to get in. Pari gently pushed Saffron's head down and covered the top of the bag with her headscarf.

"Wait here!" the little boy commanded after he took a look at Pari's grandfather. He climbed up the wooden slats of the truck and skillfully swung his body back inside the truck. After a few moments, his little body resurfaced, holding a step stool. He dropped it on the ground with a loud thud, and then took another big jump to the ground.

Pari watched him with amazement. *He jumps around like a grasshopper*, she thought. Once inside the truck, Pari noticed numerous burlap sacks of what appeared to be wheat and flour.

Once everyone was inside, Omeed pulled the tailgate back up and latched the sides. Lastly, he lowered the tarp that came down all the way, blocking most of the light. Some light came through the gaps of the wooden slats dimly lighting the interior.

"It is dark in here," Pari whispered to her mother as the truck's engine came on with a loud roar. Her mother patted the back of her hand with reassurance.

"You can lean on the sacks containing flour," Omeed's voice came from somewhere in the truck. "They are softer compared to the wheat ones."

Pari tried to focus harder as her eyes were slowly adjusting to the darkness that seemed to have swallowed everyone in it.

"Don't worry, after a few minutes you will be able to see a little," Omeed said in an encouraging voice. "I am so used to darkness now that I have a problem with light," he laughed. "My friends call me a bat! I used to get upset and fought with them until one day, I went to Pakistan." His faceless voice continued as Pari, her mother, and grandfather all listened with keenness.

"There I saw these toys and pictures of a man who wore a bat mask over his face, a black one. Just like a bat. They call him Batman and he is a Superhero!" he said with much pride.

"How old are you, son?" Grandfather's voice asked. "Where do you live?"

"I am nine years old. I used to live in the village, but now I move around a lot," he boasted. "My father was a shepherd, but he was killed in a bombing raid while herding his cattle," his voice trailed off.

"Your mother and the rest of your family?" Grandfather asked.

"They still live in the village with my sisters. I work, and take them money and food every couple of months."

Pari listened to the little boy as she leaned on her mother. The truck moved roughly as it traveled the gravel road. The darkness, the loud noise of the engine and the musty smell of the truck made her afraid. *What next?* she thought as the truck moved her farther and farther away from her village, away from everything she had known until then.

"Can I look outside, please?" she suddenly requested. "Just for a few minutes," she begged, hoping the little boy would agree.

"Just for five minutes," the boy said with an authoritarian tone. "I have to make sure everyone follows the rules. Follow me!" he said and switched on a flashlight. Omeed was shining the flashlight directly on his face while grinning ear to ear. "Follow the bat." He commanded and began to crawl on his knees toward the back of the big truck. Pari followed.

As soon as he lifted the tarp halfway, a trail of dust and cold air rushed in. The tall mud walls of the village began to shrink in size as the truck moved forward. The smoke from chimneys danced upward in a synchronized manner. It seemed to Pari that the approaching dusk in an attempt to catch the sun and drag it behind the mountain was spreading a red-colored net over the horizon. Everything looked so peaceful and serene from the far away, even the leafless trees and barren land that surrounded the village. It was deceptive, like a beautiful mirage in the middle of a desert. She remembered the kind blacksmith, the thread seller, the bird shop, and the little colorful birds that were kept in small metal cages. She was always astonished by how melodious they were in spite of living in captivity. They were hopeful. They looked at the sky every day and dreamed of freedom. That kept them alive. Just like the people of my village, she concluded.

Omeed lowered the tarp. Held the flashlight in his mouth and began to crawl back to his spot.

"Follow the light and you will be fine!" he said as he tried not to drop the light from his mouth while he spoke.

Pari froze in disbelief. Those were his father's last words that night by the window.

"This is a big truck. You might get lost." The boy said jokingly.

Pari began to slowly make her way back to her spot. Once the flashlight was turned off, she frantically searched in the bag for Saffron. Maybe he is wandering around the truck, she thought, feeling sick to her stomach.

"He is here under my burqa." Her mother quietly whispered in her ear. "He was about to follow you around. You should know better. He is like your shadow. Be careful next time." She warned her.

"What is your dog's name?" Omeed's voice pierced the silence. Pari's heart sank, her mother gulped and Grandfather sighed out loudly.

"What do you mean?" Pari answered panicking. "It's a rabbit," she sounded desperate. Pari heard her mother slapping her forehead loudly. "Dear God!" she mumbled. To everyone's relief, Omeed began to laugh. The flashlight came back on. Again he was shining it directly on his grinning face.

"Remember? I am a Batman! I can see in the dark and I can tell the difference between a dog and a rabbit!" He shone the flashlight at Saffron, who let out a muffled bark. Pari's color drained from her face. We will get thrown out in the middle of nowhere, she worried.

"You are lucky he does not bark much. Does he have a name?" Omeed asked.

"Saffron," Pari quickly replied. "Please don't tell anyone." She begged.

"Don't worry. Your secret is safe with me." He said. "I love dogs, my father had a big one. It followed him everywhere. They even died together." His voice shook and he quickly turned the flashlight off. After a few minutes, he spoke.

"Dogs are loyal friends, sometimes better than humans. Look what we are doing to each other and we call ourselves humans." He said in a somber tone.

"You are a kind young man." Pari heard her grandfather's voice.

Outside, the darkness had descended upon the freezing temperature.

Pari's grandfather moved to her side to keep Pari warm. He spread his shawl on Pari and her mother. Pari's mother fell asleep and her head began to bounce back and forth on her shoulder. Omeed was sitting quietly somewhere in the dark.

"Grandfather," Pari whispered.

"Yes, dear." He whispered back.

"It's all my fault. Please forgive me. Maybe I should have stayed home that day," she said.

"Listen to me carefully, my child. It is always best to do the honorable thing and face the consequences no matter how unpleasant they might be than to do the wrong thing and regret it all your life," he said firmly. "You did the right thing, we all did the right thing."

"But sometimes doing the right thing is not easy," Pari said in a resigned tone.

"Well, that is when courage comes in." He replied in a whisper.

The quietness, combined with the blackness inside the truck was getting frightening. Omeed was soundlessly sitting somewhere. *Maybe he has fallen asleep*, Pari wondered.

"Grandfather, do you believe in ghosts?" Pari asked hesitantly. He did not answer for a few minutes before replying.

"Do you believe in them?" he asked with curiosity.

"Yes, I do believe in them. What if I told you I saw Father that last night? He stood by the window and spoke with me." Pari closed her eyes and prayed hard that Grandfather would believe her. The long stretched silence that followed made Pari nervous. *He thinks I am crazy*, she thought. *I know what I saw, and I don't care if no one believes me.*

"I do believe you, Pari. I wish I could have seen him too. I miss him dearly." Saying that he broke down and began to cry in a muffled voice. Pari wrapped her arms around him and hugged him tightly, resting her head on his chest. She could hear his heartbeat through his old coat. All of a sudden, the flashlight came on. But this time, Omeed was not shining it on his own face. Instead, he was shining it on Pari and her grandfather.

"Anyone hungry?" he asked. "I have some bread and cheese. The last trip was delivering vegetables and some cottage cheese, and I stole some." He admitted awkwardly. Grandfather quickly wiped his tears with the back of his hands and smiled at Omeed.

"Please take the light off my face," he said, "My old eyes are bothered by it."

"That is what happens when one's eyes get used to darkness," Omeed said as he put the flashlight down.

"I hate darkness, I will never be used to it." Pari declared. "Could you please leave it on while we eat?" Pari requested. Omeed frowned and thought for a few seconds before he agreed.

"I guess so," he said, "maybe for ten minutes. Batteries don't come cheap."

Everyone devoured the cheese and bread with eagerness. Pari could not even remember the last time she ate cottage cheese. The yellow shine from the flashlight gave the interior of the truck an eerie feeling, Pari thought. The light cast massive shadows of everyone on the sacks of rice and flour in the background. Grandfather's beard appeared enormous and with every move of his head, the shadow moved in perfect harmony. It seemed like they were all sitting inside a light bubble floating in the dark. Sometimes back and forth and sometimes swaying from side to side as the truck traveled on the rocky rough road. The light went off and Omeed retreated back to his side of the truck. Pari put her head down in her mother's lap while Saffron curled up in her arms. The cold draft coming through the wooden slats was relentless and sometimes accompanied by a frightening howling sound. Grandfather lay down, putting the duffle bag under his head.

"Hey Omeed," Pari quietly asked. "Since you call yourself a bat, do you sleep hanging upside down?" Everyone began to laugh but Omeed's laughter was the loudest.

"What do you think? I might be hanging upside down right now. That is why I turned the flashlight off so no one would be able to see me!" he teased and laughed heartily. A loud banging from the driver's side jolted everyone.

"That means we need to be quiet," Omeed explained. "If we get stopped, all of you should hide behind these sacks." He said in a serious tone.

"How often do you get stopped," Grandfather asked, sounding concerned.

"It depends on the number of checkpoints and who stops us," Omeed added.

If it were not for his childish voice and the darkness that concealed his little body, one would have thought a grown mature man was talking to them, Pari thought.

"What do you mean by 'depending on who stops us'"?" Grandfather asked inquisitively.

"There are those who take bribes and those who don't," Omeed said nonchalantly. "Those who take bribes, they don't check inside the truck."

Grandfather and Pari's mother sighed at the same time and Pari began to pray as she squeezed her face deep in her mother's lap.

"What happens if one gets caught?" Pari asked after a few minutes had lapsed, but she instantly regretted asking that question. *I don't want to know,* she thought. But it was too late as Omeed's voice from the dark corner of the truck instantly responded.

"They will send you back to where you came from. I have heard different stories from refugees. Some really scary and some really sad." Omeed added in a somber tone. "Do you know what refugee means?" he asked with curiosity.

"Yes, I do," Pari said as she quickly sat up. "Someone who is running away from danger, bad people, bombings…just like us," Pari explained.

"In the hopes of getting help from good and kind people," said grandfather who was quietly listening to their conversation.

"What if they won't help us?' Pari asked with apprehension.

"Well, we can only hope they do," Grandfather replied. "Hope is all we are left with now," he mumbled under his breath.

24

Pari was sitting underneath a monstrous barberry bush. Shiny huge barberries hang from the thick branches as they caught and reflected the rays of the sun in an orchestrated manner. There were rows and rows of white tarp tents for as far as the eyes could see. The triangle-shaped tents resembled the sails of a boat and were vibrating with each gust of the wind. Pari looked down and the ground was a bright blue color. There was no grass but rough, cold blue soil. She got to her feet with panic, but all at once, the ground moved with a thunderous roar, knocking her to the ground. She reached for the branches of the barberry bush and held on to them as firmly as she could. The tents began to float on the blue ground that was rapidly turning into water. Pari climbed up the barberry bush as the big thorns tore her skin and pulled her hair. Once she reached the top, she looked down and screamed with fear. The barberry bush was floating along with hundreds of tents in the vast ocean. Pari let out another loud scream.

"Wake up!" a voice urged. "Stop screaming!" Pari slowly opened her eyes and noticed, Omeed, her mother and grandfather were all looking down at her with worry. Saffron was licking her hand with affection. She quickly sat up and adjusted her headscarf.

Sensing her embarrassment, Omeed smiled at her.

"Don't worry. This truck has heard lots of sad people cry and scream. It always makes me sad. Sometimes I prefer transporting vegetables and flours. They are extremely quiet passengers." He said with a grin. Pari laughed.

The rest of the time that was spent in the back of that dark truck was filled with worries and anxiety. Every time the truck stopped, everyone hid and stayed hidden until Omeed whistled. That was the signal to come out from hiding. Finally, one night the truck stopped one more time, and this time the driver himself unlatched the tailgate. He helped Grandfather climb down the truck and spoke with him for several minutes. Omeed sat there, holding his flashlight in an upward position like a candle, turning it on and off. He looked at Pari and her mother, who were trying to listen to the driver's conversation with Grandfather.

"He is explaining the route to him," Omeed said. "There are more checkpoints and landmines up ahead. This is where he usually drops off people." He said, sounding apologetic. The word landmines sent a shiver down Pari's spine and she looked at her mother with horror, who looked equally frightened.

"Let's go," Grandfather said, "Time to get off."

Omeed helped them get off the truck and as soon as the driver got back inside, he grabbed the duffle bag with Saffron and handed it to Pari.

"Have a safe journey," he said, "I hope you cross the border safely. Wait a minute!" he said while climbing back into the truck. He reemerged, holding a blanket under his arm. He jumped down right in front of Pari with a big thud. Pari took a couple of steps back. *A grasshopper and a bat*, she thought.

"You can keep these," he said, "It will be cold and dark in the desert."

"Thank you," Pari said, taking the blanket and the flashlight from him. "And thank you so much for keeping Saffron a secret," she said with gratitude. "He is my only friend."

"You are welcome," he patted Saffron's head with affection. "May God be with you." He then swiftly climbed back into the truck and pulled the tailgate up. Pari looked around, and the emptiness, along with the blackness of the desert, scared her terribly. For a moment, she even considered running after the truck and getting back in it. She missed her mud house, Aalia, and even the barberry bush. She stared at the rear lights of the truck as they got dimmer and distorted by the tears that were quickly welling up in her eyes. They all stood there and watched the truck slowly vanish into the night.

"We have to keep going," Grandfather said.

"But it is so dark, what if we step on a landmine?" Pari's mother asked, sounding terrified.

"I have worked on demining this land for years. I recognize the markers very well. I will go ahead and you and Pari stay a few feet behind me." He said.

"No! We stay together," Pari protested. She walked up to him and held his hand tightly. "This land has gotten used to exhaling fire and inhaling lives. The landmines are merciless. It never lets go once you step on it, not without shedding blood." He sounded angry.

"I have the flashlight, grandfather. We will be careful." Pari tried to sound reassuring, but she despised and feared landmines immensely. *They took my father*, she thought. They began to walk as the wind blew and howled pulling Pari's headscarf off her head every now and then.

Pari looked back. Her mother and Saffron were closely trailing behind. Her mother's silhouette seemed so shapeless under her burqa. It looked more like a drifting dark cloud getting whisked around by the wind. Pari thought. *She has been so quiet she must be terrified*, she thought with a heavy heart.

Pari walked close to her grandfather.

"Do you know what father told me that night?" Pari asked, but before he could reply, Pari continued. "He told me I was the bravest girl that he had ever known."

"That is right, Pari," Grandfather said, "You are."

"And he told me I should not stop chasing the light, and to never let go once I caught it," Pari said, emphasizing on the light.

Grandfather did not say anything as he continued to walk and the sound of his crutches broke the silence of the barren land. They had barely walked for an hour when the flashlight began to flicker. Pari shook it back and forth and tapped it as hard as she could. It flickered one more time and Pari looked at her mother and grandfather's panicked faces as the light dimmed, and their faces vanished in the dark.

"Oh my dear God," her mother wailed. "What do we do now?"

"We cannot move without seeing where we are going," Grandfather said desperately. "Shake it one more time, Pari."

Pari began to shake the flashlight with all the might in her body, but nothing happened. Pari looked around and froze with fear. She imagined thousands of landmines slowly coming to life as they raised their heads and stared at them with glowing red eyes. It seemed as if the black cloak-wearing desert was ushering those monsters in their direction. They stood there and could not move. Pari wanted to scream and run. You are the bravest girl I have ever known, her father's words echoed in her ears.

"Let's just sit down where we are now," her mother suggested. "Maybe wait for the sunrise."

"That is all we can do at this point. It is too dangerous to travel in the dark." Grandfather said as he struggled to lower his body to the ground. Pari helped him and put his crutches right next to him.

"Saffron, come here!" Pari yelled out with urgency. In a few seconds, she could feel Saffron's soft fur by her feet. She quickly picked him up and put him in the bag. "There are landmines everywhere. You can't be wandering off in the dark." She patted his head. Pari loved having Saffron close by. He always managed to take some of her fear and loneliness away.

They sat on the ground and huddled together. Her mother spread the thick blanket around all of them as she tried to cover them as well as she could. Pari looked down at the stone covered ground, she wanted to avoid looking around. I don't want to see those bloodthirsty red-eyed killers. *What if they are circling us? Getting ready to pounce on us?* She wondered. She rested her chin on her knees and closed her eyes.

Pari opened her eyes as she thought she heard something. She noticed a bright light in the far distance. Her heart skipped a beat. *Was that an explosion?* She wondered. There was no sound and everything was so quiet. *Explosions are not soundless,* she thought. She rubbed her eyes and tried to focus better. The roundish light was bobbing up and down and seemed like it was getting closer.

"Grandfather, Mother, look!" Pari sprang to her feet. "I see a light!" She screamed with excitement.

"Where?" Grandfather and Mother asked, echoing each other.

"There! It's coming our way! Can you see it? I can see it clearly." Pari informed them with relief and excitement. Grandfather turned around and looked hard.

"I can't see anything. Help me up, Pari," he asked. Pari helped him up on his crutches as she kept her eyes glued in the direction of the moving light. *I don't want to lose it*, she thought.

"I can see it now," Grandfather announced.

"Me too," her mother said with excitement. "What if they are the gunmen? Or robbers?" the excitement in her voice faded away.

"We have already been robbed of everything we had," Grandfather said, "There is nothing left to rob."

"It is getting closer!" Pari informed. "Hey! This way! We are here!" she screamed, waving her hands back and forth in the dark. The light came to a stop, it did not move for a few minutes. Pari's heart began to beat faster and faster with each passing minute.

Maybe I scared them, she worried. "Please, please don't stop. Come this way." She mumbled under her breath. After what felt like forever, the circular light began to move again, and this time in their direction. Pari jumped up and down with excitement. As the glowing light got closer to them, they could see the silhouette of two people behind the flashlight.

"Salaam," a voice behind the light said.

"Salaam." Pari, her mother, and grandfather greeted the strangers in an excited chorus.

"What happened to you all? Is everyone okay? Did you get robbed?" the stranger asked, impatiently as he shone the light at them.

"Well, we are on our way to seek refuge..." Grandfather began to explain, but Pari interrupted in a panicked voice.

"And our flashlight ran out of battery. There are landmines everywhere. Grandfather recognizes the markers, but we can't see without light. It is very dark. We all can get killed instantly if we stepped on one," Pari said, all of that without taking any breath. Her mother nudged her hard with her elbow.

"In that case, we can help each other," the stranger said. "I have a little map. My name is Saif, and this is my wife, Meena." Saying that he shone the light at her. They both looked like they were in their twenties. She wore a long grey coat and had a black shawl wrapped around her head that covered a part of her face too. She pulled the shawl down and tucked it under her chin and smiled at them.

"I think it is better if we continue and not waste any time, "the stranger suggested looking distressed. "My wife is a teacher, after the girls' school was torched, she began to teach a few students at our house. The insurgents found out and kept on sending us death threats, "his voice shook as he went on. "Last night, they set our house on fire as we slept. It is a miracle we made it out alive."

"It seems like everything is burning in this land. Lives, homes, dreams. We need something bigger than a miracle to save us all," Grandfather said. Looking up at the heavens, his silvery beard trembled in the wind. "Sometimes I wonder if He has forgotten about us." He pointed up at the sky. Everyone fell silent.

"Or maybe we have forgotten each other," the stranger wondered out loud.

Pari watched the stranger's wife wiping her tears with the back of her hand.

"My school was burned too," Pari said in an attempt to console the woman. "But I can read and write. My father always helped me. He was killed," she choked. "I have a storybook in my bag, but it is missing the last pages. My father said that was not necessarily a bad thing. Since that is the only book I have, every time I read it, I get to choose how the story ends." Pari stopped herself and looked at everyone awkwardly. They were all staring at her. She felt embarrassed as she looked down at the ground. She did not know why she shared all that with those strange people. But it felt good.

"Your father was right. I can tell you are a very smart and brave girl. I can see a little dog in that duffle bag too." The stranger's wife pointed to Saffron whose head was popping out from the bag. Pari looked at her with panic. They will not travel with us, she thought with horror. But before she could explain, the stranger's wife went on. "Anyone who values life and books is my hero." She smiled at Pari with affection. Pari looked at her grandfather and mother with pride. A big grin covered her face.

"We should get going," the stranger suggested. "The more distance we cover in the dark, the better." Everyone picked up their bags and looked at each other. The fear, anxiety and uncertainty hung over everyone like a dark phantom that they saw and felt, but no one knew how to explain its existence without terrifying one another.

Before they resumed their journey, grandfather, touching the flashlight with his finger, whispered something in the stranger's ear, who smiled and nodded.

"I think Pari should take the flashlight and light our path." He said as he handed Pari the light. Pari looked around and everyone nodded in agreement and smiled. Pari enthusiastically took the flashlight and shone ahead. The light pierced the darkness as its strong rays bravely cut the blackness, making a gleaming path through it. Pari looked around and imagined the fiery-eyed beasts retreat back into the duskiness of the night as their eyes slowly lost their red glow. She smiled with relief as she imagined the last scary beast vanished soundlessly. They all followed the light as Pari lit the way.

The nights turned into new dawns and the passage of time and the hardship of the journey drained them of their energy and willpower.

Pari stayed determined and hopeful as she dreamed of living in a world that was kind and loving, a world that helped one catch the light and keep it forever.

Also by Zahra Omar Shansab
The Shoeshine of Kabul